Y0-CCH-775

Comments & Reviews for previous book
By Anita L. Allee: **Closed, Do Not Enter**
1857-1865 Missouri and Civil War

"The best book I've ever read," eighty four year old female reader from MO.

"I enjoyed the story as well as the inspiration. It is nice to read a good up-lifting book for a change," Dee E. from KY.

"My husband read your book in two days, he especially liked the Civil War part." Wife from MO.

"I stayed up until midnight reading," a male reader.

"I'm so proud of your work," retired teacher.

"I cried when I saw your book on the shelf. I knew it was your dream," young mother.

"I could not lay the book down until it was finished," CA reader.

Many readers commented on their male and female Civil War era ancestors and the hardships war brought upon the families. Several Orphan Train descendants also wrote.

Future titles: *Back Country Adventure*
Historicals: Yankee Spy in New Orleans
Who's the Boss
Two Together
River Run

**Missouri Center
for the Book**

ༀ ༀ ༀ

**Missouri Authors
Collection**

MAC
FIC
ALL

Child of the Heart

Anita L. Allee

Historical Novel
Set in Old Franklin
&
Boonville, Missouri
1824

Copyright © 2003 by Anita L.
All Rights Reserved
Cover Painting by Mary King Hayden

ISBN: 1-59196-398-2

Published in US by Instant Publisher.com
PO Box 985, Colliersville, TN 38027

This is a work of fiction based upon scant truths. Characters and events are embroidered on the following true facts: a young male teacher came to Missouri from Kentucky. He was divorced. He later married one of his students. She fell into the Missouri River, was kept from drowning by the buoyancy of air captured under her willow hoop skirts. The couple purchased a child on the river front in St. Charles, Missouri. The child when bathed was not black.

Ultimate design, content and editorial accuracy of this work is the responsibility of the author. Scripture references are paraphrased by the characters from the King James Version of the Bible.

Publisher's cataloging-in-publication
Allee, Anita L.

    1. Early Missouri history at Franklin and Boonville, Missouri. 2. Christian life and history.
   Fiction-title

All rights reserved. No part of this book may be reproduced, stored in a retrieval system, or transmitted in any form, without prior permission in writing from the author, except as provided by USA copyright law.

PRINTED IN THE UNITED STATES OF AMERICA BY
InstantPublishers.com
Contact at: anviallee@earthlink.com

DEDICATED TO ALL TEACHERS,
THOSE WHO HAVE TAUGHT
PROFESSIONALLY,
OR THE ULTIMATE TEACHERS:
PARENTS, FRIENDS, MENTORS
AND PERSONAL EXPERIENCE.
THANK YOU.

Message to the readers:
Please understand that some words used in this text
are the vernacular of the era and used to express
the personality of a character, but not words one
might wish to use.
Thank you for your understanding.

Child of the Heart Characters:

Douglas Sidwell Charlton	Professor and Teacher
Sally McDonnell	Scheming Young Woman
John Williams	Prosperous Franklin, MO, Farmer
Martha Williams	Wife of Farmer
Lydia L. Williams	Farmer's Young Daughter
Sarah Long	Lydia's Lifelong Friend
Elizabeth Sidwell Charlton	Douglas' Mother
Ruth "Addie" Curry - Girl Slave Child, Purchased at St. Charles, MO	
John William Charlton	Douglas Charlton's Son
Adrian Simms	Boonville Storeowner
Kirk Simms	Store owner's Son
Currys	Fraternal Grandparents
Bickfords	Maternal Grandparents

William Becknell and Christopher "Kit" Carson, historic figures of Santa Fe Trail fame, are used in this story of Franklin and Boonville, Missouri. The action covers the Years 1824 through 1840.

Child of the Heart

1824-Married?

I, Douglas Charlton, take up my pen to vent my anger in a more gentlemanly fashion. *Divorced*! *My calling is ruined*! I'm only twenty and I've gotten my life into this mess. How could this happen?

I married Sallie McDonnell because I was bewitched. She blinded me with her demure beauty, but she deceived me.

We drove to Louisville on our wedding night and she *locked me out*! I thought she was scared and would get over it. I thought she was pure and that made me care for her even more. I put notes of love and consideration under her door each day.

After a week of not talking to me, she asked me to come into her room, the first time I'd seen the door unlocked since we arrived with her servant after our wedding ceremony.

"I need to tell you something," she said.

She seemed unsteady and fearful. My heart went out to her. *She's such a frightened baby*. I spoke first, attempting to allay her fear.

"Don't you want your girl to leave?"

"No, she knows what I'm going to tell you and I need her here."

I can still hear her words ringing incessantly, in my head.

She seemed out of breath, "Before I became— *attached* to you, I was secretly married to a man you don't know and— you don't need his name. I'm carrying his child. I'm sorry that I had to go through a ceremony with you to get away from my parents. I have no intention of staying here with you. It's all been arranged, he'll come for me on Monday and we'll leave together. You won't have to bother with me again. Thank you for helping me get away from my parents."

I was so taken back, that I lashed out at her in anger.

"Why did you do this to me?"

"I was desperate and you were acceptable to my parents."

"You made a fool of me. I'll never be able to stay in Kentucky and teach school again. Communities won't have a divorced man. You've taken my love and my livelihood— trampled it in the dirt!" I wanted to hurt her, as she'd hurt me.

She looked at me in a detached and cold manner.

"You're good looking with your black hair and dark eyes— you're personable. You have family money and a southern heritage. You'll have no trouble finding a *good* girl who fits in with your family and who loves you for yourself." She was re-hearsed, trying to excuse what she'd done.

"But— how could you?" I asked.

"What I've said is the way it is with us. Accept it— get on with your life."

"You've thought it all out, haven't you?"

She stiffened in her chair, turned away, and looked out the window. Dismissing me, she had determined her course, she had worked out her communiqué, now she had delivered the message and didn't show remorse. *Finished! She was finished with me.*

"How could you have been so calculating?"

With no more to be said, I left and went straight to see a lawyer. I thought Louisville was far enough away from home that my family and community wouldn't see my humiliation. I was already here. I wanted to get this thing over.

That's when I purchased this journal and started talking to myself through the pages. I wrote and wrote, venting my anger on the pages of *Jay* as I started to call the journal in my head. He wouldn't reveal my secrets and I was too humiliated to talk to another person. My head began to understand, but my heart hadn't recovered.

After three months of languishing, feeling sorry for myself, and depleting my financial supplies, I acquired my divorce. *Divorced, from what?* A real *fiasco*. I was angry. I thought of other things I could have said to her, but I knew it was better I hadn't. She caught me so unexpectedly that I was personally hurt. I couldn't bring myself to say it then, and now, I can't bring myself to write the words I thought.

Finally, I convinced myself to imagine her desperation. Had she not deceived me, I am sure we could have made a match, as I did care for her, maybe not love, but the beginnings.

I worked at odd jobs and finally came to a decision. I'm leaving here, I think I'll go down the Ohio River and drift along until I can find some place, or work that suits me.

<hr/>

"Thank you for taking me on. I wish you well," I told my latest employer as I packed up to leave his inn on the riverfront where I'd worked as clerk.

My outlook improved as I drifted from job to job, and place to place. Three months later, I arrived at Franklin, in the relatively new state of Missouri, on the north side of the Missouri River. It was the spring of 1824.

I found a job at the livery stable; it was interesting enough. I had no obligations to anyone other than myself and Franklin was becoming the starting point for westward travel and a destination called the Santa Fe Trail. Franklin was the second largest town in Missouri and provided rich opportunities for many itinerant laborers.

I met interesting characters passing through the area. They frequented the stable as they waited for the trading caravans to move west in the spring. I met farm workers who needed temporary jobs for cash money; drummers peddling their wares; Indian scouts; guides; young and old settlers; all sorts heading west.

I'm writing less and less in my journal, but bring it up to date on occasion, as I am now.

In the late afternoons during winter, I was bored. I went to the general store. The customers sat around the warm stove telling tales and passing time.

Before the river froze over in December, the town shut down with the cold. I purchased ears of popcorn from the store owner. We shelled the popcorn and I put it in a gallon bucket with some lard. I punched holes in the lid, then mashed it on the pail. The pot-bellied stove glowed cherry red as I sat the bucket on the top. The sound of that corn popping drew men like flies to honey. More and more fellows drifted over. I salted and shared my corn with those sitting around the stove on the benches, nail kegs, and chairs. I had to let the bucket cool before I could reload it, but we ate five gallons of popped corn that first evening.

In the friendly conversation, it came out that I was a teacher. One man approached me to teach him to read. He was waiting for spring to break, so he could make a trip on the Santa Fe Trail. The second evening, he brought along a friend. Soon we had *friends of friends*, until I had seven men learning to read.

A youth who was apprenticed to a saddle and harness maker joined the band. He didn't wish to study, but enjoyed the stories of the men of their adventures and travels. The more stories they told, the more interested he became. He was always the last of the *scholars* to leave.
He was an interesting lad.

One evening he told me his father had been killed when the limb of a flaming tree fell on him. I deducted that his father was in his sixties when he was killed and the boy only nine or ten years of age. His aging mother struggled to support the children who remained in her household. Kit had been apprenticed as an early teen to assist his mother and gain support for himself.

The young man seemed at loose ends and couldn't wait until he was old enough to have the adventures of the rough bull whackers and mule skinners of the Santa Fe Trail caravans. I became attached to Kit, filling the role of an older brother for him. He stopped by the livery stable during many of his deliveries for his mentor.

I used a slate, because the school books were too childish to interest these rough men.

During our store classes, we wrote our own stories from the tales we heard around the fire during the evening. The storekeeper pulled down the shade and locked the store each evening at six. He agreed to leave us inside.

After we finished our studies, I banked the fire for the night and turned out the lantern.

As each evening progressed, I made a list of what we ate and left payment in the drawer. Cheese, crackers and pickles were our mainstay for supper the rest of the winter. One of the men brought a bucket of milk some evenings and we passed that around with our store food.

Travel became busier in January and February when the river froze and more horses came to the livery stable. When I was delayed with my work, the men gathered and began without me. When they heard my boots on the porch, they opened the door and let me in. Often I didn't get there until well after dark.

Only Johnny and Kit of the first group of men were left when the wagon and pack trains moved out in the early spring. He and I recruited another class and started over. By now, he could help with the beginners, while I'd teach the more advanced scholars, with Johnny included. The new class practiced writing their names or simple sentences on slates while those who had learned to read recited.

By the end of that summer, the town of Franklin, and Boonville, south across the river, had become accustomed to me. Judged by my actions, I could tell they assumed that I was not a fugitive from justice. I had a good recommendation from the owner of the Santa Fe Trail Livery Stable, the storekeeper, patrons and the owner of the boarding house where I lived, and my class members.

An opening became available in Boonville for a professor at the young men's and young ladies' academies. My teaching credentials were impeccable and did not have *Divorced,* emblazoned across the front. I was hired, but I did not reveal *all* my past history to the head master.

My first year was uneventful, filled with the usual school activities and settling into the routine. I had missed the academic circle and the scholars since leaving my home and job in Kentucky, but I found, *now*, I also missed the society of men at the storefront school in Franklin.

On Fridays, I ferried across the river for a visit. I had a standing reservation for a sleeping room at the boarding house and spent Saturday teaching and visiting in the back room of the store.

On Saturday evenings, I rode across the ice or caught the ferry across the river and spent Sunday in church, and with the Sunday events at the Academies. Many of the scholars boarded between holidays and I helped chaperon.

I was occupied and didn't find time to write in my journal often. I caught up when I had an afternoon of leisure. I could read that my mental health was better than it had been at the peak of my anger, I no longer needed my journal as I had previously. I used it to help me think when important decisions came. My journal seemed to help as I spelled out details in black and white.

Strictly Forbidden

My second year at the Young Ladies' Academy, I met Miss Lydia L. Williams, a young lady not easily dismissed from one's mind. She had long strawberry blond curls, the bluest eyes, and a sparkle. She often got into trouble for her bubbling exuberance, which her maturing young body seemed unable to contain.

We male teachers were required to remain aloof from the female scholars and keep proper demeanor. We were allowed to associate socially only with our fellow teachers and the adult community, with close scrutiny of our activities at every proper social event in the community. If we wished to be less than mature and keep the proper decorum, some traveled far away. Our behavior must remain exemplary to keep our academic positions. Mine met these standards. Fraternization with scholars was strictly forbidden the male, or female teachers.

I'm back to my journal to voice thoughts I must not express orally. I find it more and more difficult to ignore Miss Lydia as the year wears on. She seems everywhere I look, or maybe I am searching for her. She makes me feel— marvelous.

I have to admit that I am a little shy of the fairer gender after my experiences with *Sallie McDonnell*. I have stayed clear of females for almost two years. Young ladies must win their way into my confidence after that episode.

I never intended anything to come of my interest in Miss Lydia, for she is only fifteen years old, but her beauty and spirit intrigue me. I can't help but see her scholastic abilities as she studies in my classes with her female classmates and socially with the boys. *Very proper, but with a special spark always there.* She's a center of attention at the academy.

ᴥ

The more time I spend in class with Miss Lydia, the more fascinated I become. She is the epitome of honesty, a trait I didn't find in Sallie.

As I attend school events, Miss Lydia is in the forefront of all activities in her social group. Just blossoming into her feminine beauty, her cheeks glow with rosy health. She makes it hard to miss her when I go about my academic duties. She is *good* and caring, but not *too* good. I enjoy life and do not enjoy spending time with those who are sour or overly *self-righteous.*

At a spring lawn party, I met her father. We visited and I found that I liked the man. He carries some of Miss Lydia's enthusiasm and Mrs. Williams has passed on her coloring. Both parents are intelligent and polite.

There are three brothers in the family, even though I have only the two older in my classes. One is older, and two younger than their fair, damsel sister. Mr. and Mrs. Williams' philosophy of child rearing appears to be that their children are impressed to do all they are capable of doing and shaped with proper balance.

As I observe, I can see that they don't hold Miss Lydia back in her being reared with brothers. Perhaps this explains her ease with female scholars in academic pursuits, and male scholars in mixed social events.

I catch myself noting that Mr. Williams is somewhat older than Mrs. Williams. I brood on that subject. Why does the age difference in Miss Lydia's parents come to my attention? I can deny it no longer, *I have an interest in Miss Lydia that is not strictly professor to scholar.* This is against my whole philoso- phy, as I am extremely conscious of the possibilities of exploit- ation by the older party in a teacher scholar relationship. I have witnessed in some teachers, but strictly avoid, even the ap- pearance of favoritism on my own part in my classrooms.

ᴥ

This summer, I am in a dilemma. *Leave? Pursue my interest in Miss Lydia and therefore, give up my teaching position at the Academy?*

I have spent from March through July at the Santa Fe Trail Livery Stable, mulling my situation. I must come to a decision soon, the school term is to begin in October and I am no closer to a solution than when the term ended in February.

I observed the family coming and going to town as I, again, teach the men. I will seek Mr. and Mrs. Williams when they come to town next Saturday. I will arrange my schedule to *accidentally,* meet them at the general store. The family lives on the north side of the Missouri River above Franklin. They frequent Wyan's General Store most often when in town.

᠅

October: Late afternoon on Saturday I went to the store, as usual. When Mr. and Mrs. Williams arrived, I gave them time to make their purchases and then stepped out the front door on his heels as he followed his wife outside.

I remember our conversation vividly: "Mr. Williams, I'd like to speak with you, if I may?"

"Professor Charlton. Certainly. What can I do for you?"

"Let me help you load that first, Sir."

We stepped to the rear of his wagon and shoved his purchases in the back over the tailgate. I purposely stayed in the street, so we would not be overheard during our conversation.

I rushed into my prepared oratory, "Mr. Williams, I've noted the special qualities of your daughter during her time at the Academy. I'd never do anything to disrupt her academic pursuits without asking your permission first. I'm interested in her personally and would like your permission to see her socially. I hope you see my situation. I *can not* stay on as a professor at the Academy if I see her socially. I assure you, I will not make my interest evident without your permission. I can stay on at the Academy, everything as usual, or I can quit my job and see Miss Lydia? It's your and your wife's decision."

Mr. Williams had paid rapt attention to all that I said, but I was unable to read his expression. He looked away for a moment, up and down the street. He turned to look directly into my eyes and then looked away again.

"This is unexpected. We've seen no signs of your interest."

"That was my purpose, the outward appearance I had to convey," I replied.

"I'll have to discuss this with my wife. I don't have an answer for you now, Professor Charlton. I do appreciate this talk before you acted. Some men would be less responsible and considerate of our family and the community's feelings."

"I am aware of the difference in our ages. I am twenty-two years old and I know Miss Lydia's age is sixteen. I work with her records everyday, but I have also noted that in this community, often the man is somewhat older than his wife. Please don't mention any of this to Miss Lydia, but before you make a final decision, I need to talk with you and your wife further."

"I appreciate your keeping your interest quiet- it might effect Lydia's academic pursuits, if she knew of your interest." He looked away, "Especially, if we should dis-approve your suit. We will give you an answer next Saturday."

Mr. Williams climbed aboard his wagon. He sat there for a time studying my face; he gathered the lines and backed his team from the hitch rail. Mrs. Williams studied the two of us. He turned for a final look and nodded as they started down the street out of town. The couple appeared in ardent conversation as they passed. I touched my hat, and stood where Mr. Williams left me, until they turned the corner and disappeared from my view.

Favorable? Unfavorable? I have no way to know, but he didn't get angry or immediately say, *No*. I took a deep breath, my legs were shaking. I felt lighter, turned on my heel, raised my knees high to unobtrusively shake them loose, and went into the store to socialize around the cold stove. I didn't hear all the conversation, I found myself distracted.

Parental Intervention

I fidgeted, as I awaited Mr. and Mrs. Williams' decision on the next Saturday, I couldn't calm myself.

Finally, I saw Miss Lydia's father and mother coming down the main street toward the store. It was unusual for them to come to town two Saturdays in a row, without other family members. I was sure they had made this arrangement purposely. They turned into the hitch rail and alighted.

After Mr. Williams wound the lines around the brake, I stepped to his side of the wagon and waited, my hat in my hand. Mrs. Williams looked down as her husband extended his hand and spoke.

"Professor Charlton, can we go down to the river park for our discussion?"

"Certainly, I'd prefer a private place, as I'm sure you both would. Would you like refreshments while we talk?"

Both shook their heads. Mr. Williams placed his hand under his wife's elbow, helped her from the buggy and guided her down the street toward the river.

I turned and walked behind Mr. Williams. I tried to stay calm, but I felt an inward quiver of dread. When we reached a grove of trees on the river bank, Mr. Williams seated his wife on a bench under a tree. He and I quietly stood in the shade, we formed the remaining two corners of a triangle.

Mr. Williams earnestly looked at me and then smiled. I felt more encouraged, but knew that I must reveal more inforation to them, before they gave me a final, possibly favorable decision. My revelation might cause them to withdraw their consent because of my status as a divorced man.

"You must have other information about me before you make your final decision. It wouldn't be fair of me to allow you to decide without revealing something more about myself." I withdrew my legal papers from my pocket, along with three letters from my home county in Kentucky.

I spoke quickly, to prevent any reply before I could speak.

"I must explain this paper before I give it to you, so that you can understand the circumstances. This is a divorce decree. It is mine, however the marriage was never legal. I was drawn into a situation and after a week of being locked out of our room, my bride revealed that she was already married. She never intended to live with me. She went through the marriage ceremony with me in order to get away from parents who disapproved of the man she had married. She left the next day and I've never seen her since. We were in Louisville, so I had a lawyer file a divorce for me."

Both the Williams were stunned.

"Professor Charlton, why didn't you just have the information removed from the books, if the situation was as you described?" An intelligent question from Mr. Williams.

"That would have been the proper thing to do. I know that now, but my lawyer and I were young. I was stunned and hurt, didn't know proper procedures. By the time I learned differently, the divorce was final. I wanted out and I didn't go back to have the marriage esponged from the records. I didn't realize the possible consequences at that time."

I handed him three letters, "Here, these other three documents may explain further. One is from a minister that has known me much of my life. In fact, he's the man who performed the ceremony. Afterwards, he apologized for not counseling us further. We both should have been more discerning. He has a good reputation in Kentucky, if you'd care to contact him."

I handed the papers to Mr. Williams.

Mrs. Williams shook her head and reached to shove them away, "I'm not sure this is any of our business, it's your private matter."

"No, if you will consider my wish to see Miss Lydia socially, you have a right to know everything that might cause you to be uncertain about my intentions. I know that she is honest and I can be no less and be a man about this. I'd like to forget the whole episode, but that's impossible. It's on the books and open to anyone that might chance to examine the records. It might prove an embarrassment at a later date and I wouldn't be satisfied if you didn't know the whole truth." I was out of breath.

"Professor Charlton, we need time to consider. Would you be so kind as to leave us for a few moments?"

"I'll return in a half hour. You can examine the papers, then I'll retrieve them. You may not have a decision in a half hour, but take all the time you need to consider my proposition. I'm sorry about this divorce, but I'm afraid it does have a bearing on our situation."

I tipped my hat and walked away. I couldn't go back toward the store and the gaiety of the men. I walked out of town to the west. I didn't want to meet anyone. I glanced back from a rise. They were huddled on the bench and I had an impression. *They are praying.*

When I reached the furthermost point that I could walk back in the allotted time, I bowed my head in prayer.

Dear Lord, Help me to accept your decision. Help me to accept the Williams' decision and be content whatever that might be. You have an answer, I don't. I'm beginning to care a great deal for Miss Lydia, but that will have to be put aside or maybe—have to wait. In my Savior's will. Thank You, Amen.

I walked with eagerness back to the bench under the shade tree. I had to know the answer, even if it was negative.

Mr. Williams turned solemnly, as I neared. Mrs. Williams looked at my face and then down again.

I spoke first to make it as easy for them as I possibly could. "I've prayed and I'm willing to accept your decision, if you have one?"

Mr. Williams spoke for the two, "Here are your papers, Professor Charlton. We can tell that you've been very honest with us."

Mrs. Williams asked in a faint voice, "Did you love the girl?"

"I thought I did."

"Were you willing to stay with her and make it work."

"Yes, that was my plan."

Mrs. Williams nodded at her husband.

He spoke the words I wished to hear, "We are favorable to your suit—"

I started to thank him, but he held up his hand to stop me.

"Under certain conditions— you must wait another school term before you make your intentions known to Lydia, and your actions must continue to be exemplary. If you prove yourself, abide by these conditions, and still wish to see Lydia after the school term dismisses in the spring, then we will grant our permission for you to see her socially, but only if she agrees."

Relieved, I replied, "You couldn't be more fair, I accept your conditions."

I was elated. The wait would be *easy*, I had become accustomed to waiting. I solemnly shook Mr. Williams' hand, bowed and doffed my hat to Mrs. Williams and received the first smile I'd received from her.

"We'll see you around town and at school functions. Take care of yourself. We'll be praying for you," she whispered.

I thanked her, guided them back to the store and excused myself. This was one day that I would savor in private. No reference on the subject would escape my lips to others, until the end of next February. I began formulating plans for further talks with the parents Williams, but nothing unusual to Miss Lydia.

Excruciating, Enduring Promise

I anticipated the school term would go quickly and be joyous as it always had for me, but I found that it *ground* along. I couldn't believe that these months could go so slowly. Miss Lydia was more vivacious and beautiful than ever. She made my life miserable while waiting to be near her, as other, than her teacher.

I observed Miss Lydia and her friend, Sarah, riding away, as they left school each day with a swarm of young men. I found myself giving the group more attention than was necessary. I hate to write this, but I saw her as the center of attention as the day students left with their horses each afternoon. A green-eyed monster speared my heart as I watched the gaiety of their departure. I'd give anything to go riding with her. What if she's smitten with someone else before I get a chance to reveal my feelings to her?

Some of the students found me distracted and commented. "Professor Douglas, you must be getting old and deaf."

I joked with them, but I knew the reason and they didn't. I chastised myself. *I need to be more careful and not neglect any scholar, or duty that is given to me at the Academies.*

I've withdrawn from the camaraderie at the general store because I fear in a weaker moment, one of the men might learn my secret. They torment me unmercifully.

"You're becoming a stiff old bachelor."

"You need to find a woman and settle down." *My exact feelings.*

Christmas is near. Today I was invited to partake of Christmas Dinner with the Williams family. It is not unusual for a teacher at the Academies to spend some holiday with one or another of the families, but I thought better of it and made excuses to this family.

Later, I privately sought Mr. Williams to apologize for my inability to attend. I explained in order for me to remain neutral, I must decline an immediate in-vitation. He understood and thanked me for my candor. This is the way I remember our conversation.

"I thought perhaps you had decided that you no longer wished to see Lydia socially?"

"No, that couldn't be further from the truth. I must stay away from her socially, or I might reveal something you don't want. I only have a few more months, surely you can understand my dilemma? I appreciate the invitation, but I think my refusal is for the best, under the present circumstances."

I spoke in warning, "Don't ask me after the February term, *unless you intend for me to come.*"

Mr. Williams smiled in reply and shook my hand, then turned from me to speak to the visiting minister.

⚋

Spring Disaster

The late winter rains came. On Monday, the second week in February, disaster struck. Douglas heard a cry go up from the resident scholars.

"She's lost! Her horse came limping back to the ferry alone."

"They trailed the horse back from where she got off the ferry, then found the river bank caved in before she got in sight of the school."

"The flood waters undercut the road and when she rode over it, the road gave way and fell into the river. They can't find her!"

Oh, God, don't let it be Lydia! That's selfish of me, but that's the way I feel. I have to be honest, please don't let it be Lydia.

Douglas and the scholars ran toward the river road to join the crowd already gathered. Half of the road was gone and the water swirled into the cut.

"Move back! There may be more under-cutting. Move further from the water. Move back." Douglas moved the young people to safety and then walked as close to the edge as he dared.

"Are you sure she's in the water? Have you walked the bank down river?"

"We *have looked*, we didn't find anything. Take the boys and look on your side down river to the east. We'll cross on the ferry and look on the north side of the river."

"Who is it?" Douglas asked.

"We don't know, they just said a girl from the Academy was in the river and her horse came to the ferry limping and wet. We didn't hear which one."

"Girls, you go back to your dining hall. Pray and have the cooks prepare warm food for everyone. Have the housekeeper warm blankets near the fire until we bring her. We'll be back as soon as we can. Go, hurry," Douglas directed.

He watched them until he was sure they obeyed, then moved the boys and gave them instructions.

"Divide into twos and walk the bank. Don't get too close without being sure of your footing. You know how traitorous the river currents are. It's swift and we'd have trouble getting anyone out. One of you walk closer to the edge and the other further up on the bank. Grab a long pole and keep it between you, that way, you could be saved, if you do slip. Yell if you see anything at all. Look for places where she might have climbed out."

"Boys, let's pray before we begin. Dear Lord, keep these young men safe and keep the lost girl safe and well. Help us find her as quickly as possible. In Christ's name, Amen."

Douglas continued to pray as he walked ahead of the front two boys. *I must set a good example, even though I want to jump in and swim along to look for her. Oh God, please don't let it be Lydia.*

Who else rides to school on Monday morning?

He ticked off in his mind the girls who rode horseback to school. *Lydia rides with Sarah. If one of them fell in, the other would be there to help, or maybe they both went in and only one horse got out. Oh, God, this is worse than ever! Help us all.*

I must calm myself and try to think of the girls who ride. My mind is a blank.

The further the men walked, the more he despaired.

Night came. The sky grew dark. Torches lit the banks as they stumbled along. Finally, a wagon picked up the cold, exhausted searchers along the river roads.

"I can walk further, we can't stop! Bring lanterns, we can keep going," Douglas pled.

"Lantern light doesn't extend out far enough, we'd miss too much area."

The men conferred and general agreement reigned.

"Professor Charlton, we can't see any longer. You could walk by her and never see her. We can't afford to have anyone else lost."

"It's too dangerous at night. We'll continue the search in the morning," another agreed.

"Everyone must go home. Get dry and get some hot food inside yourselves. We'll meet before first light and be ready to take up the search at dawn in the morning."

"I'm afraid none of us will rest tonight. Let us pray before we disband. We'll place her in the Lord's hands," the reverend spoke quietly.

All gathered in a circle with bowed heads, most too overcome to speak.

Two of the students became more frightened by Professor Charlton's mood.

"He's sure taking this hard."

"I know he likes us, but I didn't know he cared that much about us," whispered the two. They huddled closer together to keep their emotion in check. Professor Charlton's dejection weighed their spirits.

The boys devoured all the food set before them. Professor Charlton drank coffee only, then more coffee. He shivered uncontrollably and the searchers were concerned for his health.

"Professor, you got too much exposure today. I'll send up hot water. You go get a

hot bath and try to get some rest?" the matron insisted.

"Do you know which girl was lost?" Douglas asked.

"Why yes, it was Sarah Long. I thought you knew?"

"Lydia...?" He covered, "Uh, Miss Lydia's friend, Sarah Long?"

"Yes, go ahead and get some rest. I'll send the water right up."

"Well, where's Miss Lydia, I haven't seen her all day?"

"She was ill this morning, so she's home in bed. Sarah was riding alone. Maybe that was a blessing or we'd be looking for two girls instead of one."

"Yes, you're probably right." Douglas turned, his back straightened.

Matron watched him as he walked away.

He whispered, *Thank you Lord. I know I'm being selfish, but I thank you that she was sick today. Amen.*

An old Negro servant knocked on Professor Charlton's door, then opened it quietly and prepared the bath.

The professor was nowhere in sight.

Douglas didn't want anyone to see his face. Overcome with thankfulness and sorrow from the day's happenings, his dirty face would reveal his emotion.

"Master Douglas, you in there? Your bafwater's hot."

"Yes, I'll be right there. Thank you. Go on, it's fine."

Sorrow and Rejoicing

Today, I retrieved my journal. Theses thoughts are too painful to reveal to the scholars or anyone else in the community.

We all spent a miserable week. Today they found Miss Sarah Long's body. She washed up on the roots of a huge sycamore tree in an eddy down river. The cold temperatures preserved the evidence of a horseshoe shaped bruise on her temple. She had been injured in the initial fall with her horse into the water. It was determined that she was knocked unconscious and drowned without possibilities of getting herself to safety.

The two academies will close for a week of mourning.

When classes resumed, a final push began for graduation and closing ceremonies.

Douglas saw Miss Lydia having difficulty when she returned to school without her lifelong friend. The two girls had shared most of their life's experiences. He felt the strong desire to scoop Miss Lydia into his arms, comfort her, and tell her how happy he was that she survived and was well. He turned aside for a moment to gain control of himself. When he turned back, he was his usual helpful self, caring for the obvious needs of his scholars.

"Miss Lydia, we're glad that you're well. Can I be of help?"

She gave a stricken look and quickly dropped her eyes. "No— go on as usual. I'll be fine."

That evening Douglas dug out his journal to write his thoughts:

During the day, it was difficult to see her struggles. Some
times the tears brimmed and ran down her cheeks, but she asked
for no special attention. Both academies were subdued and went
quietly about their work. They avoided the mention of the
thoughts uppermost on their mind, for fear of further break-
down in themselves or others.

Despair is contagious and each of us has a good case.
Young or older, none of us were immune to this disease.

At the dual graduation from the two academies, a special recognition was given in memory of Miss Sarah Long. The President of the boy's student body offered a prayer in remembrance of her.

"Dear Lord, as we remember Miss Sarah Long, make us better for knowing her. We pray that her family will be comforted and help us to remember the good that she did. Bless us all in this loss and keep us close to you. May the memory of her good qualities continue to influence and cause us to be better citizens. Amen."

Several class members sniffled quietly before raising their heads.

Lydia sought out her teachers and classmates. Douglas watched her progress toward him.

"Professor Charlton, I won't be coming back to the Academy next year."

His heart quickened. "Are you sure that's what you want to do?"

"Yes, I'll miss the Academy— and all of you, but I think it's time for me to get on with my life. Without Sarah, it's not quite the same. Thanks for all that you've done for me. I wish you the best next year and in your life."

A part of Douglas cried out in pain for Lydia, and another part in elation for himself and what might develop between them without the confines of their present relationship as professor and scholar.

Now I can tell Lydia how I feel and I'll be able to help her— in other ways. I must go see her folks first, get final permission before I tell her. At her home, away from the academies will be a happier, easier place for us to start a new relationship. I'll move across the river today after final closing ceremonies at the Academies.

He packed his belongings and moved across the river to the Franklin Boarding House for the spring and summer. He made plans to work at the Santa Fe Trail Livery Stable, expecting availability of time to court Miss Lydia. Living on the same side of the river as Lydia's family would make visiting the Williams' farm more convenient.

Going Courting

At the livery stable, Douglas harnessed his favorite driving horse. He climbed aboard and drove to the Williams' farm. As he came into sight, Lydia raked windfall sticks from under the trees in the front yard. She didn't expect callers, or recognize him. She disappeared into the house, as he rounded the end of the yard fence. Tying his horse to the hitch rail in front, he walked to the porch, knocked on the door.

Mrs. Williams answered the door. "Why, Professor Douglas, we've expected you. Come in."

"Is Mr. Williams here? I wanted to discuss past decisions with him."

"He's in the barn. Let me get my jacket and I'll show you where. Go around the side and I'll be right out."

Douglas walked to the side of the house. He wondered where Lydia was keeping herself, but he needed to see her parents privately, first.

Mrs. Williams came out putting her arms into her jacket. Douglas held the back of her coat for her, then seated it on her shoulders. She buttoned it against the cold. He put his hand under her elbow and steadied her as she walked toward the barn through the thawing mud.

"I walk this everyday. You don't have to impress me further, you can let go. I can make it fine."

"I'm sorry, I didn't mean to imply you couldn't. I like to help people and you're the closest right now." They both laughed.

Douglas glanced back toward the house to catch a curtain moving over the kitchen window. *Someone inside wonders what's going on.*

He couldn't keep a smile from his face as he turned back toward the barn.

"Paw, where are you?"

"Here in the corn crib, I'm cleaning the last of the winter's corn out for the stock."

"Professor Charlton is here about our agreement. Can you come out in the open?" Mrs. Williams fanned the air. "It's dusty in there."

Mr. Williams came out, dusting his hands on the sides of his pants.
He held out his hand to Douglas.

"Professor Charlton. Wondered when we'd be seeing you? Kind of figured you hadn't forgotten after the way you looked when Sarah was missing."

"That was an extremely hard time for all of us at the Academies. I didn't know who we were looking for at first, I was afraid it was Miss Lydia. I'll have to admit, I was relieved when I heard she was home, indisposed. That was one time when I was grateful for an illness."

"We were glad that she had to stay home that day. We don't know what would have happened, but it must have been the Lord's will that she not be along with Sarah that day. It's a tragedy for the Longs, but we can't help being grateful for Lydia's safety."

"I still want to honor our bargain, if you'll let me?"

"You've more than lived up to your part, we can't say any different now. We do appreciate how you've conducted yourself. I don't think Lydia has even a hint of your interest," Mr. Williams commented.

Mrs. Williams nodded. "I couldn't help feeling favorable after our discussion last summer and when I saw how you helped the young people with Sarah's death. I'm glad you'll be here to help Lydia adjust. I think I'd better go tell her that you've come to visit her and we've agreed. You men visit here out of the wind for a few minutes."

As Mrs. Williams left, Mr. Williams leaned his tools against the wall.

Douglas fidgeted, paying only half attention to his comments.

"Been a long hard winter for us with Sarah gone. Last week, we had three cows struck by lightning under that cedar tree. I hope things go better for the community the rest of the year."

"You're right."

"I'm looking forward to getting into the fields before too long."

"I'll be working at the livery stable again. I probably won't teach any of the men this summer, because I want to see Miss Lydia on Saturdays. If that's agreeable with you, Sir?"

"Yes, that's fine with her mother and I. You need to ask her, she may have other ideas. We advise and encourage, but I'm not making this decision for her. She's the one that you'll have to convince, not me."

"Sure, I just meant, if I'm not in the way?"

"Her work will be done by Saturday afternoon, evenings belong to her, she can do what she wants with them. If it suits her, you can go to church with us and eat Sunday dinner here, but don't accept on my account. I'm being friendly, but not begging to be rid of my daughter. Please recall her tender age."

"You surely know by now that I'll treat her well, and it will be her decision. I love her, but she's probably never thought of me in any way other than her teacher."

"Oh, you might be surprised. I overheard her and Sarah talking under the covers. The girls at the Academy think you're quite the fellow."

"Mr. Williams, they're imagining that. You know I've never encouraged any of them." This topic of conversation embarrassed him.

"I know that Professor, but young girls come easily under the spell of their young men teachers. I've admired the fact that you didn't take advantage of it. I'm hoping you'll keep to that high standard." Mr. Williams looked seriously at Douglas, "Don't you trifle with my daughter."

"You have my word on it, I'd never do that to Miss Lydia."

"Okay, Son. The same feelings hold true for all youngsters. My sons aren't immune to the charms of their female teachers either. That's part of the job of being a teacher, letting a little hero worship give them an example that they can look up to. That's why it's important for the adults to be honorable in their dealings with the youngsters. My sons have been in your classes too. They have a way of talking about their teachers. If a teacher gets out of line, they are quick to let us know."

"That's one of the reasons I admire Miss Lydia. She and her brothers show love and concern for each other. That's a good family example that they've learned somewhere. Your family is one of the most honest that has ever come into my acquaintance. I've never heard one of your children tell something that I felt was anything but the truth, however they are not *unkind* with the truth. Like the Bible says, ". . .their mouths, and hearts are free of guile.""

"We're proud of our whole family, they're growing up the way we want them to. We're all believers too. I know you go to church at Boonville. Are you a follower of Jesus Christ?"

"I certainly am. It's very important to me, I wouldn't seek out a wife that wasn't a follower of my Master."

"Glad to hear that! You better get on up to the house, or Maw and Lydia'll be wondering what I did with you."

"Oh, I guess we kind of got our subject broadened, but I'm glad we did. Thank you, Mr. Williams. I hope to be seeing you often."

Douglas turned toward the house and put his hat back on his head as he walked across the yard. He stepped up on the front porch and removed it nervously.

Mrs. Williams met him and held the door open, as she motioned him into the empty parlor.

Questions

"Where is she? Did you tell her?" Mrs. Williams nodded.
"What did she say?"

"She'll give you an answer. Right now, she's getting ready. I expect she'll be down in a few minutes. You can't come calling without giving a girl notice, now can you?"

Mrs. Williams turned to the cook stove. "Would you like a cup of coffee or something while you wait?"

"No, I'll just sit here and relax until she shows up. How are the boys? Are they home today?"

"They're fine and working on the farm somewhere. They'll be surprised to see a professor at their home on a Saturday right after the Academies turned out for the term. They may not even like it. Don't get me wrong, they like school, but they're glad spring has arrived. I think they'll make themselves scarce when they find out who's here. I'll get back to work, you enjoy yourself 'til Lydia comes down."

Douglas did *not* enjoy himself. He was too ill at ease. Just as he hadn't shown his feelings to Miss Lydia, she hadn't shown hers to him, now he doubted his appeal to her. *To her, I'm old.*

He heard a light tread on the stairs as Miss Lydia approached. He stood quickly and twisted his hat in his hands, waiting for her to enter the room and speak first.

"Professor Charlton, we're glad to have you visit our home. Won't you sit down? Did Mother offer you some refreshment?"

Douglas was speechless. *She knows why I'm here and she's as calm as can be. Doesn't she know how nervous I am? Well, here goes.*

"Miss Lydia, I'm sure your mother told you why I'm here. I know it may be a shock to you, and you may need some time to think it over, but I'd like to know if I might call on you?" He was out of breath.

Sarah answered, "I've never kept company with anyone, but I think I would enjoy it. We've always gotten along well at school. I'm acquainted with your character. Mother told me about the conditions that you agreed to last summer." She looked at his hands working his hat. She glanced away and straightened her spine with new confidence.

He spoke, "I waited almost a year to ask you if I could call on you, so it's not a new thought to me."

"I was surprised that you asked, but it bothered me that you or my parents didn't tell me about it before. None of you dropped so much as a hint. I had a little time to think while I got ready. If I'd known before, I'm sure someone might have guessed. Now that I'm out of school, I think it's probably better to have waited."

"I was pleased to have you in the Academy, but it made seeing you easier when I knew you wouldn't be coming back under my tutelage. I offered to quit my job, if you had stayed on next year."

In surprise, she forgot herself, "Oh, I wouldn't have wanted you to quit, that would have made your calling on me impossible. I'd never want to come between you and the Academies. You're too good with the scholars and teaching to quit."

He smiled, "I'm glad you appreciate my teaching, because I feel that I am *called* to teach, just as some are called to preach. I've been able to make a difference in a few lives and I'd like to continue that, the Lord willing."

"And you *should*. If a person has a call from God, they shouldn't let *anyone* stand in their way."

"I'm happy for your understanding. Now, would you like to take a short ride in the buggy or would you rather stay here in your parlor?"

"It's late in the day, I'd just as soon stay here. Mother said that I could ask you to Sunday dinner tomorrow. Would you like to come? You could come, go to church with us too."

"Maybe we had better let your family digest these new happenings before we spring it on your church and the community."

"That does sound reasonable. I need a little time to adjust too."

"That's fine, I'll come be with your family for dinner, but I'll go to church in town tomorrow, if that's agreeable with your family? You can tell your brothers I'm coming, then they won't be too shocked when I show up."

"That will be fine, we are in no hurry on Sundays. We won't get home until about twelve thirty or one, so you'll have time to drive out from town."

"Well, I'd better get the horse back to the stable. I'll see you and your family tomorrow." Douglas turned back, "Maybe we can take that buggy ride tomorrow afternoon?"

"That would be fine. The weather looks promising for a fair day tomorrow," Lydia remarked.

"March is a little erratic sometimes, but the sky is clear now. I'll see you tomorrow. Good night." He stepped to the front door and let himself out. Lydia followed.

Standing in the door, she waved as he got into the buggy. He looked back to see her quietly close the door and saw her mother through the window.

Douglas drove away with happy feelings bouncing in his head.

I think that went well. I can't expect a huge outpouring of immediate affection when I just sprung it on Miss Lydia. I got a big boost from Mr. and Mrs. Williams, and their comments made me feel even better about my decision to come courting. Thank you, Lord for   everything that was said and done. I'm pleased that the family carries you in their hearts and feel the importance of Christ in their lives. I knew Miss Lydia and the boys were Christians. I know they had to have an example somewhere, I think I've found their source today. It's a wonderful family— I pray that I can be a part of it, if You're willing.

New Beginnings

Douglas joined the family for the noon meal on Sunday. Afterwards the brothers and Lydia invited him outside.

"Professor, you want to join us in a game? Lydia likes to play. We've got a hand carved cedar bat and old shingles for bases," Joseph, the fourteen-year old stated.

"I've never played this kind of ball, but if you've got the proper tools, I'm sure I could learn. By the way, out here, I'm just one of the fellows, don't treat me special."

"We'll try not to mess up your fine suit. You should bring along some old clothes, usually we get a little dirty around here," prompted Harold, Lydia's oldest brother. "We play a game we read about in a New York paper in Boonville."

"I'll hang my jacket on the porch rail. Now, can you show me what to do?"

"Since there's five of us, two of us will strike at once, while two take the field. Harold will feed the ball and the striker will try to hit it. If the striker hits it in front of him, he runs counter-clockwise around the three bases and back to where he started. When you're in the field, you can catch him by soaking the ball at him. If you hit the runner, he's out," David explained. "When you hit the ball and someone catches it, you're out."

"Whoa, you've lost me," Douglas chuckled.

"You'll catch on. Harold feed the ball to me and you can see how it's done." Being the youngest, his family deferred to him often and let him talk, because he hadn't always been able to do everything the older family members did.

Harold fed the hard little ball at David, who swung the long thin bat. *Whomp*. He hit the ball. It sailed straight up and landed behind him.

"I don't get to run unless it lands in front of me." He picked up the ball and tossed it to his brother. "Here's the ball, feed it again."

Whomp. The ball sailed over Harold's head and landed in front of Lydia. She grabbed it up and threw it at the running David. *Pop*. The ball hit David in the shoulder.

"Don't spare me, Lydia! You about took my shoulder off!"

"I'm sorry, but *you're out!*"

Douglas was surprised at the strength and skill with which Lydia hit her brother with the ball. *This family is not easy on its own members, however there is plenty of love shown.*

"Come on, it's my turn to strike," Joseph hollered.

Harold fed the ball and Joseph hit it into an empty spot. Douglas picked it up, tossed it at Joseph, but missed.

"Don't hold back, he's tough and he's still going," Harold ran to retrieve the ball where it had fallen. By the time he was in position, Joseph had stopped on the third shingle.

"David, you're up to strike again."

"I know, I know, can't you see I've got the bat and am standing here waiting on you? Feed it up here."

This time David connected and sent the ball into an empty place near the second shingle. Douglas hurried to retrieve the ball and threw it at him. Joseph ran home.

"You can throw it at either of the runners, whichever is closer, or you think you can get the best. Now they have one out and a run. Joseph, it's your turn again." Harold brought the ball behind his head and let fly. Joseph struck, but missed and David advanced to the second shingle. Joseph retrieved the ball and smacked it into Harold's hands. Harold blew on his hands, but gave no other indication that his hands stung.

The second feed went high. David advanced to the third shingle, while Joseph again retrieved the ball. Mr. Williams came out on the porch and then walked behind the striker.

"I'll get the balls behind the striker for you."

"Strike it hard! Joe, bring me in!"

Harold wound up a bit harder and zinged the ball toward Joseph.

Joseph swung and sent a high flying ball to the middle of the field. Lydia ran to retrieve the ball and threw it at him. She missed and Joseph continued on to the second shingle. David ran into home when she made her throw at Joseph.

Lydia got Joseph out on David's second attempt and now the striking team had to hit around again before the team in the field succeeded in getting the third out to advance to striking position.

Lydia and Douglas went toward home shingle.

"You strike first, so I can see how you do it," Douglas directed.

Lydia looked self-conscious. Harold sailed two balls past her before she showed her irritation.

"Feed it higher." She *lammed* the third feed over his head, took off for first shingle and got there before David was able to soak at her.

"Okay, it's your turn to strike, Professor. I'll give you two practice swings before they count, so you can get the feel of the bat. It wouldn't be fair to you, if you don't get a little chance to practice. Where do you want your feeds?

I don't know, just feed it up here and maybe we can decide."

Harold fed the first pitch, very slowly. Douglas over-anticipated the ball reaching him and struck too soon.

"I'll feed it a little harder this time, that should help you and the ball get together."

Douglas swung and caught a piece of the ball. It bounced on the ground in front of Mr. Williams, and then ricocheted.

"You got a little of it. I'll throw it back to Harold, so you can try again. You've about got it now. You might try to keep your eyes on the ball as it comes toward you, other-wise you won't know whether to hit high or low."

"Okay, I'll feed this one about the speed of the last and it counts. Don't forget to run, if you hit it in front of you. Lydia, here's for real, you can run now."

Harold fed the ball into the area where Douglas had been striking. The ball hit the bat and dropped in front of him.

"Run Professor, run! It's in front of you," Mr. Williams instructed.

Harold ran to retrieve the ball and tossed it at Douglas. He missed and the ball flew past Douglas' leg.

"Keep running." Lydia rounded third and headed for home. Harold threw at her the last few feet, but missed.

"Lydia, you strike again and get the Professor in this time."

She was getting over her self-consciousness and knew that the Professor would be busy running, rather than watching her. She drew back the long bat and slammed the ball over Joseph's head. He backed to retrieve the ball, as she dropped the bat beyond home shingle and ran to first, then second shingle. As Douglas ran into home, he looked back to see where the ball was and stumbled on Lydia's bat.

"Whoa, Son, you're about to get down there," Mr. Williams reached for Douglas' arm to steady him.

"Thanks, I'd better watch where I'm going next time."

"Get me in this time," yelled Lydia. And he did.

Douglas ended up on second shingle and Lydia made an out when Joseph hit her with the ball going from second to third. Douglas rounded third and ran for home. Joseph retrieved his throw as Lydia waved her arms to distract him from his throw at Douglas.

"That's not fair. Don't cheat Lydia." They both laughed.

Harold caught Douglas' next hit and Lydia went to second. When David missed her, his throw rolled into the ditch and he had trouble finding the ball. She ran to third.

Douglas knocked the ball over his head. Harold caught it.

"Three outs, it's our turn again," yelled Joseph.

"Okay, Harold, it's your turn to play now. Step on up and

I'll feed for awhile," Joseph said.

Douglas noted that the family wasn't easy on each other, but were good sports about the game.

The sun baked down and the younger people's faces grew red. Mr. Williams wore his Sunday straw hat to shade his face.

"I think Mother has made some lemonade, why don't we stop and get a drink," said Lydia."Papa, you thirsty?

"Yes I am, Daughter, why don't you go get the pitcher and glasses? We'll meet you on the porch in the shade." The men walked to the water tank and washed their faces and hands before they came to join her.

"If I have you fellows at school next fall, it will be the same as usual, I'll be the teacher and you the scholar, we'll have to act as if we haven't rough-housed together. Hope you can understand and not hold it against me?"

"Yeah, but we'll get you good this summer, because you'll get us good next winter," Joseph bragged. They laughed, all very relaxed.

Mrs. Williams came out carrying the pitcher and Lydia came with the glasses on a tray, wet strands of hair sleeked back from her face. The men took offered glasses and Mrs. Williams filled each one, beginning with Douglas, then Mr. Williams. She sat the pitcher on the wide rail and Lydia leaned the tray against the front of the house. Mr. and Mrs. Williams sat in the swing, Lydia in the rocking chair and the boys sat on the steps. Douglas leaned on the porch rail.

"That's a fine game. I enjoyed myself. You young people aren't too easy on each other, but I guess that's the way families are. My brother is competitive and we were a little rough and tumble too. Our only sister died when she was two with pneumonia. I can hardly remember her, as I was only four myself."

"We're very sorry you lost your sister, Professor Charlton. Are your parents and brother still in Kentucky?" Mrs. Williams asked.

"Yes, my brother lives close to my parents. He and my father farm together. They ship a little timber on the side."

"Has your brother ever taught school, like you do?" asked Lydia.

"No. We went to a seminary for young men, but when we graduated, he was finished with school. He said he'd had enough education for the kind of life he wanted to live. He immediately went to work with our father. Of course, we'd both been working with him as soon as we were old enough."

Douglas continued, "In Kentucky, we raise tobacco and a few acres of cotton, so we learned about hand labor very young. Rob is four years younger than me. He's always been a farmer at heart."

"We raise flax and hemp here along with the usual Missouri crops of wheat, corn and oats. It's not the best climate for cotton or tobacco, but some folks raise a little," commented Mr. Williams. "The season is sometimes a bit short between frosts."

"I never liked raising tobacco. My father didn't smoke and we weren't interested, so it was sold for cash. A tobacco crop requires a great amount of hand labor and the tobacco worms were a menace. That was one job I was glad to leave, when I left Kentucky."

"Why did you come to Missouri?" asked Harold.

"I've told your parents the main reason I came and I'll let them explain that to you later. I was ready to move and I wanted to teach again. I could do that as well in Missouri as I could somewhere else. I think the people here around Boonville and Franklin are more interested in education than they were in the county where I grew up. I'm really happy with my jobs at the Academies. They are better positions than I had in Kentucky, *and* I met your family, I have *you* for scholars. That's hard to beat."

The family chuckled.

Harold looked puzzled.

One by one, the boys drifted off the porch to other pursuits.

"Martha, think I'll go take an afternoon nap."

"I'll be inside, in a bit. You go on." Mrs. Williams

gathered the tray of glasses and the pitcher. Douglas held the door
for her. She turned and spoke through the screen.

"You young folks have a good buggy ride, or swing here
on the porch. If you need some more pie or lemonade, it'll be
under the table cloth, help yourselves. We'll have a cold supper
in a few hours, make yourself at home."

Lydia stayed in the rocking chair, but turned toward the
swing when Douglas sat down.

"Your family is very comfortable to be with. I don't know
when I've enjoyed myself more."

"We've been glad to have you."

"Thank you for inviting me. You certainly don't have to
feed me this evening. I shouldn't take up your whole afternoon."

"No, that's fine, we don't do much on Sunday
afternoon—a lazy day of rest for us and our animals. It's about
the only day that my folks take a nap, but my brothers and I read,
play a few games or laze around outside most Sunday afternoons.
Sarah used to come over, or I would go to her house after church
sometimes."

"You miss her, don't you?"

"Yes, since I don't have a sister, we did sisterly things
together. I don't have any other girl friend that I feel quite the
same about or who lives as near. We could run up the road on our
horses, or walk and see each other everyday if we wanted to."
Lydia dropped her head and was quiet.

Douglas didn't know quite what to say. He looked down
and when he looked back up, he saw a tear trickle down Lydia's
cheek. She turned her head and looked away toward Sarah's
home.

Before he thought, he rose and knelt in front of her. He
took her hand and spoke.

"I'm so sorry you lost your friend. I've never had a close
friend die."

Lydia looked down at his hand holding hers.

He looked into her face and whispered, "I thought it was
you that day. It scared me so I could hardly stand it. I didn't find
out who was lost until we searched all day. When we got back to

the Academy, Matron told me when she sent me to rest. I was relieved to hear you were sick in bed. I thanked the Lord for your safety."

Lydia raised her head and looked into his face. More tears brimmed and rolled down her cheeks. Douglas stood to search his pockets for his clean handkerchief. He unfolded it and put it into her hand. She rose and turned to wipe her eyes. He reached to put his arm around her shoulder, but lowered his hand without touching her.

"I'm sorry, I should be over Sarah's death by now, but it hits me at odd moments. I don't know what made me think of her now."

"I think it's only natural because you spent so much time together. Any little thing that you once did together, can recall memories of other times and happenings. That's bound to go on for a long while. After a time, the memories won't be so painful, but you will remember your special friendship with more joy than sorrow. You'll never forget her, but become glad that you shared with her for the time you had."

It was natural for Douglas to raise his hand to Lydia's arm.

"Sarah was a Christian, like you, so you *will* see her again one day."

"I know, but thank you for reminding me, sometimes I miss her so, that I forget about seeing her later." Tears started again.

Douglas drew her closer and she rested her forehead on his chest. He patted her back and left his hands there.

Finally, Lydia collected herself and stepped back. She wiped her face with his handkerchief, refolded it and put it in her pocket.

"I'll wash this for you tomorrow. I'd hate for you to use it all rumpled. Thank you for reminding me that I'll see Sarah again, that makes me feel better."

"Why don't we go for that buggy ride now? I'll get the horse out of the barn and hitch her."

"That would be fine. I'll go tell Mother where we're going and wash my face. Do you want a drink or anything before we go?"

"No, thank you. I ate enough of that good Sunday dinner to last me awhile yet."

"I'll get my bonnet and be right out."

~~~

Summertime and the Livin' is Easy

During the late summer, Douglas kept his eyes open for his own horse. The year before, a young sorrel gelding with a white star in his forehead had come back with Mr. Becknell's stock from the Trail. As the young man cared for the animal, the horse rumbled in communication Douglas as he fed, curried, and mucked the stalls. He gave the *red* special attention.

"Mr. Becknell would you sell me that red sorrel gelding we keep in the second stall?"

"You can use him every time he's in, you don't have to buy him. He's a good one and wouldn't come cheap. "

"I'm serious about Miss Lydia and I want to start thinking about a family horse. I like that one, he's dependable and I'd like to have access to him when I go visiting."

"So you finally found the girl did you? Are you getting married?"

"I haven't asked her. I'm not sure how she feels, but she's the one for me, if she'll have me."

"That's good, the Williams are a wonderful family. I think you'd be happy together. Tell you what, I'll do you a favor and put a price on the horse. Let me look up what I paid for him and I'll get back to you this afternoon."

Mr. Becknell waited until Douglas left the office, then picked up his account book. *Hum, that's a little steep. I'll just alter that figure and give Douglas a quarter of the horse as a wedding gift.*

While Douglas closed the livery for the evening, Mr. Becknell waited for him at the front door of the stable.

"Here's a bill of sale with the gelding's price. If you still want him, that's my price. I can sign it when you make a decision."

Douglas glanced briefly at the figure, "I'll take him. I don't spend much of my earnings and I have some in savings. I'll bring it to you in the morning. Thank you, Mr. Becknell. I think he's worth more than this. If this is what you paid, you got a bargain and I'm willing to pay more."

"When we got him in Kansas, he wasn't well-trained, he's come a long ways since I picked him up on the way home from Santa Fe. Asundry folk treat horses differently. A livery stable is a good place to find out the disposition of animals, because they have to put up with inexperienced riders and drivers. If the horses remain sound in body and disposition under those conditions they are dependable in most anything you can put them to. As you know, we break them for harness and to ride, so they're well-rounded horses once we get them going good."

"I know he's a good one. Customers pick him out again after they use him once."

"Okay, I'll see you in the morning when you come to work. I'll have to find me a replacement all-around horse. Thanks Douglas for being a good, dependable worker. I wish you the best in your courtship with Miss Lydia."

"Thanks? I need to thank you for many things, including this job and the sorrel horse. You believed in me when I didn't know anyone else in this town." Douglas offered his hand to Mr. Becknell and they shook mutually, then clapped each other on the back. Douglas walked away whistling. Becknell smiled as he rounded the corner on the way to his office.

ख़

Early in the summer, Douglas went to visit Lydia every Saturday evening and spent most of the day Sunday with them at church or in their home. Part of the couple's time was spent with the Williams family and part alone in various recreational pursuits. Douglas went fishing, played ball, then he and the brothers went to the swimming hole on the creek one Saturday evening.

At first, he visited only on weekends, but soon came on Wednesday evenings too. It became harder and harder for he and Lydia to be apart as their feelings for each other spiraled.

At the formal parties on the lawns in Boonville, the young ladies wore white summer dresses and big hats. Their escorts wore suits and straw hats. Some of the activities were less formal when they went to play parties.

They bobbed for apples and the men ended up getting thoroughly wet. Southern influence was strong in Boonville and Franklin.

They attended cotillions, which some called quadrilles after the four couples participating in each square.

Church affairs were attended as a family, including a brush arbor meeting on the riverbank at Franklin.

By the end of the summer social events, the two communities had become accustomed to Miss Lydia and Professor Charlton appearing as a couple and ceased thinking of them as *their professor and his scholar.* Their relationship with the communities and each other was very comfortable.

"Would you like to become engaged in the fall for your birthday? I've asked your father and he said that he'd give me your hand in marriage, but he'd like for us to wait until spring to be married. That is if you say *yes* to my proposal, of course."

"What are you asking? You'll have to put it in words for me, I want to be sure I understand what you're saying."

"Yes, Lydia, I know you, you want it spelled out. I love you, will you marry me?"

"Oh, Douglas I love you too. I will marry you." Lydia gave Douglas a big hug and reached to kiss him on the tip of his nose. "I'd like to be engaged on my birthday and it will be fine with me for us to be married soon after the Academies close at the end of February. How's that for an answer?"

"Wonderful. I'll write my parents to get ready to come to Missouri for a March wedding. This should give them time to get themselves organized and get here on time."

"Oh, yes, I want to meet your family. I've heard so much about them; I feel I already know them. That small painting you showed us lets me know that they look like you. I'll probably recognize them when I see them, because you and your brother look like *stiff* twins in that portrait. I can hardly tell which is which."

"You're laughing at our portrait? You know the painter made us stand still, but mostly Mother made us be rigid. We probably wouldn't have looked so much alike. I think when you see them in person, you'll be proud of your new in-laws, you know how much better I look than in that painting."

❤

Douglas purchased a ring with a blue sapphire for their engagement. He nervously placed it in his pocket on the evening of Lydia's birthday and drove impatiently to her home.

Lydia heard the clop of hooves and ran to meet him on the front porch.

"Happy Birthday, Sweetheart." He alighted, tied the gelding to the hitching ring and greeted her with a kiss. He held on. "Close your eyes and give me your hand." He placed the ring on her ring finger.

Lydia opened her eyes.

"Oh, it's beautiful. How did you ever know that blue was my favorite color?"

"I've observed what you wear and your eyes match this stone. Go look in the mirror and check."

"Oh, they're not quite that bright a blue, are they?"

"Yes, sometimes. They change. Sometimes they are very blue and other times, they're clear and lighter. You'll have to look more often in various moods. You probably don't see yourself like I do. When we dance, your eyes are deep blue and excited. When you cry, they look like a blue lake. When you say you love me, they're happy and sparkly. Then sometimes you're calm and they're like a blue sky in Missouri during the month of October, crisp and deep. They're never the same twice. I love you however they look." He teased, "I haven't often seen your eyes when you're mad, so I don't know how they look then. You look in the mirror and see sometime."

❧

The August Academy opening was very hot. The scholars languished and had difficulty buckling down to work. Some of the hottest afternoons, the Professors and teachers took them out to the shady lawn under the big oak and elm trees.

Male or female classes were under every tree on the spacious rolling lawn that lay between the two schools and ran down to the river. With the water in view it seemed cooler, even if it wasn't. Those of the opposite gender were a mild distraction for the older scholars.

Douglas missed Lydia from his classes, but accepted her new position as his fiancee and former scholar. She was now a grown woman, with a new status. He recognized her distancing herself from the academy scholars more and more as the term worn on. She acquired a mature confidence in his love.

The couple wrote to his parents in Kentucky at Christmas and asked them to come to Missouri for their March wedding. They impatiently awaited the arrival of a reply from his family. Slow in coming, when the letter did arrive they were in for a disappointment.

"The letter says that Mother has had a respiratory ailment this winter. That was why she was slow with their reply. They won't be able to make the trip for the wedding, but they invite us to come visit them at home this summer."

"I'm sorry they can't meet my family and see where you work, but I'd like to go to Kentucky."

"We'll go right after we get married. That would give us about a month to travel and three or four months to visit Kentucky and the family scattered there. How's that?"

"Oh, Douglas *can* we? I want to see your home, where you grew up and meet your family."

"That would be wonderful. I have plenty saved, so I won't have to work this summer, we'll make a grand tour of it. We can take along our riding horses and a pack animal on one of the big keel boats on the Missouri River. Then we can ride part of the way cross-country."

"There's much to see in Kentucky and I want to show you all of it. The river trip would take up the first part and we can honeymoon onboard. Maybe we could even take our guests onboard and have a party for them before we let them off at Jefferson City or somewhere up the way. They can have some-ne meet them with their buggies after the party and drive back the next day. They could stay the night at the Lohman Tavern. How'd you like that?"

"That sounds too good to be true. Do you really think we could do that?"

"Why not? We could probably find a boat and manage."

"Oh, let me go tell Mother and Daddy. My brothers will be as excited as I am."

When Lydia returned with her sparkling eyes, Douglas had new ideas to present.

"I'll talk to the landing office and find the best date and boat for our party. We'll
work out the details and make the arrangements as soon as we can, so we'll be assured of room on the boat for our guests."

When Douglas returned with two possible dates and details, Mr. and Mrs. Williams drew him aside.

"We want to pay for the boat trip. It will be our wedding present and send-off for you."

"That's not necessary."

"Yes, but we want to do it for you and Lydia."

"Please allow us to enjoy doing this for you both," begged Mrs. Williams.

"If it's what you really want to do, that's fine with me. Talk it over with Lydia and if she agrees, we'll go ahead. Do you have any different ideas for the celebration? Discuss it and if you wish to speak to the shipping company, I can introduce you to the folks I talked with, or you can look for different ones."

Their trip was set. Douglas' red gelding and Lydia's own sorrel mare, Ribbon, along with Mr. Becknell's pack mule from the livery were in the corral at the landing. The saddles, bedding and bags were packed and stowed aboard in one of only two private cabins on board. Douglas secured the cabin by speaking early to the company. Party arrangements were made directly by the Williams.

The wedding was set for three hours before the boat was due to leave, and the food prepared and ready. The wedding party and the congregation of friends and relatives were gathered in the early afternoon at Lydia's church. The minister stood before the crowd..

"Would you please stand for prayer?"

Lydia and Douglas could remember very little of their ceremony.

Rev. Peters said, "You may kiss your bride!" before they realized they were married.

Douglas *did* kiss his bride and they turned to greet well wishers. They moved out of the church with the crowd and to Douglas' rooming house for final preparations.

Lydia's mother packed her wedding dress and assisted her change into a ball gown with a willow hoop skirt for the party. They picked up Lydia's luggage and her mother gave her a final hug. The two went to meet Douglas.

"You look wonderful, *Mrs. Charlton*!" He took her bag in one hand and her hand in the other, pulled her close and gave her a peck on the cheek. They both laughed and stepped out the front door in their party clothes.

Refreshments were laid out on the veranda of the boarding house. Most of the congregation stayed to send off the newlyweds.

As the keel boat loaded, the small crowd jostled. The Williams were ready to climb aboard. Excitement filled the air. As the boat prepared, her crew started to load the last minute baggage and animals. Lydia and Douglas walked the send-off line to thank those who were not going along for the ride and party. They moved toward the river to board.

A plank lay from the dock to the deck of the large flat boat. Members of the party walked the precarious connection. Lydia waved when she stepped onto the plank, the current shifted and the plank buckled. Lydia was caught unaware and tumbled into the treacherous currents of the Missouri River. Her mouth flew open in shock and her quick intake of breath took in the cold river water. Her pink parasol bobbed to the surface, then her head, then all disappeared. The next time she appeared, she was sucked away by the swirl of the current around the boat, her skirts ballooned about her.

Douglas frantically ran down the deck to the rear of the boat in an effort to catch Lydia. Before he could reach her, she was gone in the wake of the boat.

Oh God, no! Don't let this be like Sarah.

He leaped back onto the dock; passed the deck hands, who were becoming aware of the accident.

One porter directed, "Man overboard. Grab the hooks! She made it past the rudder, but she's movin' away. Lower a boat, get a boat. Hurry!"

Douglas grabbed the reins of the nearest horse from the hand of a porter, grabbed a handful of mane and leaped to the animal's back. Seizing the reins next to the bit, he drew the leathers over the head of the animal and dug his heels into its belly.

The horse slipped and scrambled for footing as it slid on the boards of the ramp.

Douglas slipped to one side, but grabbed a handful of mane and clung in desperation. The startled horse reared before it leaped in the direction of the river road. Douglas lay over the animal's neck urging him on after the pink bit of fluff that could occasionally be seen on the surface of the river. He was gaining as he prayed to reach Lydia in time.

"I'm gaining, hang on, hang on Lydia! I'm coming!"

Dodging limbs that hung over the edge of the road, he stayed as close to the river as he could.

A mile, two miles. He rounded the bend where the current swung into an eddy, ahead of Lydia, and skidded from the animals lathered back. His legs buckled and wouldn't support him. Diving into the water, he came up within a dozen yards of Lydia's ballooning skirts. Five quick strokes and he clutched her dress, pulled her to him and raised her head from the water. She coughed and took a shuddering breath of air.

"Lydia! Lydia, are you all right?"

He heard only choking and retching, holding her head above water, he hit her between the shoulder blades. She coughed again.

"I've got to get you out where I can help you bend over and get rid of this water. Hang on, I've got you."

Lifting her to the shallow gravel bar, he attempted to stand up in the water. Their clothes weighed them both down, but he succeeded in wrestling her to dry land. Upright in front of him, he bent her over his arm with her back to him and pounded on her back. Lydia coughed and choked. She gasped for air and tried to speak.

"Relax, it's fine now, I've got you." *Dear God, I've got her, thank You.* "Come on Lydia, breath, breath, don't try to talk, just breath!"

By this time, the crowd had started to arrive. Mr. and Mrs. Williams arrived in a borrowed wagon and leaped to assist Douglas and Lydia up the bank. Someone shoved a blanket into Mrs. Williams' hands and she helped him wrap a shivering Lydia in its warm folds.

"Here baby, we've got to get you warmed and out of these wet clothes," Mrs. Williams soothed.

Mr. Williams placed a coat around Douglas' shoulders and guided them to the wagon. He cleared his throat before he could speak.

"Let's get these youngsters back to town and changed. They need to warm up. Harold, catch that horse and take him to the stable for a good rub down. Notify his owner and make what restitution is needed." Mr. Williams continued, "Let's get moving. Ride on ahead and tell the crowd that everyone's safe. Have them get somewhere warm ready for them and get some dry clothes off the boat. We'll be along as soon as we can."

Mrs. Willliams nestled Lydia against her and patted Douglas' arm.

"You did well, Son. I prayed all the time you were gone. I

thought I'd never see her alive again. Thank you," her voice choked off.

Douglas looked at her in understanding. Realization flooded over him and he shivered anew.

Mr. Williams turned to look at the trio in the back of the wagon. He turned to wipe his eyes and then spoke to them.

"We've seen the treachery of these currents," he hesitated to clear his throat. "It's something we've lived with ever since we moved here. Not too many survive a fall into the Missouri River. Thank you, Son, for saving our daughter. She's in good hands, *yours and the Lords.* God Bless you, keep her safe."

After hot baths at the boarding house, Lydia and Douglas seemed no worse for their dunking. Lydia, Douglas and her parents sat together drinking hot tea in the dining room. Lydia coughed occasionally, but had stopped shivering.

"I'm ready to go to Kentucky. Is the boat still here?"

Douglas spoke softly, "Sweetheart, are you sure you want to try it today? You swallowed that river water and you might— take a cold or have some ill effects. I'm a little shaky myself. Maybe we should stay here for a few days and take up our journey when you feel a little stronger."

"My throat feels a little raw, but I'm ready to go now. All the crowd is still out there and I don't want to keep them waiting. Mother and Daddy paid for everything. We'll have all week to rest. Let's go."

"The Captain said they had a doctor aboard, so I guess you can get as good care there as here. Mrs. Williams, do you think Lydia should go today?"

"I'd advise against it, if I had the decision to make, but you are married and I'll not make that decision for you."

"Mother, I'll see the doctor on board and I promise you that I will rest and take care of myself. I'll be happier if we go ahead as planned. I want to remember the good things today, not what happened just now."

"Okay, close up your bag."

Lydia's father reached for the second bag, "I'll carry it outside for you and Douglas can get his. Let's get you safely aboard this time."

The crowd cheered when Lydia and Douglas appeared. They patted the couple as they passed.

"Are you all right?"

"How are you Miss Lydia?" "You look good."

They reached out to touch her, as if to reassure themselves that she was fine. Some patted Douglas on the back and said how pleased they were about his heroic deeds.

Douglas kept his hand around Lydia's elbow and turned to the crowd as they neared the boat.

"Lydia wants to go on to Kentucky. There's a doctor on-board, so if she needs further care, he can assist us. The ride is still on, so everyone that is to come aboard be careful. Thank you for helping us celebrate Lydia's safety and our wedding."

He handed his and Lydia's satchels to a dock hand, then got a firm grip on her elbow. The deck hands had laid the animal ramp with rails from the dock to the boat. Lydia held the rail with her one hand. Only Douglas noted her white knuckles as she hitched her hand along beside her.

Mr. and Mrs. Williams followed so closely that they could touch Lydia and Douglas as they moved across the ramp. No one was taking any chances of further incidents. Mrs. Williams carried the sodden ball gown. It would be restored for Lydia to wear in Kentucky.

ॐ

The Wedding Party was a huge success with celebratory fervor. The banjo player and the colored quartet were quiet, but beautiful. A waiter served a tray of tiny sandwiches, drinks and desserts to the family gathering.

After two hours, exhaustion began to show in Lydia's face.

"Daughter, let me take you to your cabin and help you get settled."

Lydia nodded and looked at her mother blankly.

"Douglas, Lydia has agreed to let me help her get settled, we'll be in the cabin."

Douglas watched them as they walked away. Mrs. Williams had a firm hold on her daughter's arm.

In their cabin, her mother laid out a white lawn gown with tucked bodice on the quilt and turned to move Lydia toward the bed.

"You'll be aboard for a week, so I'll put your things in the cabinet. You go ahead and get into your night gown and I'll sit with you until Douglas comes."

Lydia moved lethargically through her bedtime ritual. Her mother tucked her into bed and sat brushing out her long hair. Lydia closed her eyes and sank further and further into the downy pillows. Martha stroked her daughter until she went fast asleep. She bowed her head and prayed silently for her daughter and Lydia's new husband.

Oh Lord, thank you for sparing my daughter today and providing her with a man that would risk his own life to save her. Keep her well and travel with them. Give them both the strength to make this trip. Keep them safe and don't let anything bad happen to them. I pray that she will love and be loved by her new family. Help this marriage to be successful. Bless them and help me let her go. Thank you. May they both be in your will. Amen.

Tears ran silently down Martha's cheeks. Lydia rested comfortably. Both were at peace as Lydia's mother continued to look at her only daughter as she slept.

When the boat stopped at Lohman's Landing at Jefferson City, Douglas and Mr. Williams came to the door of the cabin. The two men conferred quietly outside. Hearing their voices, Martha kissed her daughter on the forehead and left the lamp turned down to a soft glow in the wall sconce. She went to the door and opened it. Mr. Williams looked in the door at his daughter and seemed satisfied. He shook Douglas' hand and hugged him with the other arm.

"Thank you, Son. God bless you both," and turned to leave.

Mrs. Williams stepped outside the door and hugged Douglas.

"She seems to be fine, she's just tired. God bless you both. Thank you again. Take care of her for us. Take care of yourself too. We all love you both." She gently pushed him in the door and softly closed it behind herself.

John and Martha Williams walked away with their arms around each other.

"He'll take care of her, she'll be fine, Mother."

"I know. I don't think we could have found a better son, had we picked him ourselves. I feel good about their choice. We have to thank the Lord for them both."

"I have."

"I have too," she squeezed her husband as they stopped for an embrace.

The Williams gathered with their sons, at the back of the small crowd going down the gangplank. They would rest at the landing's tavern and drive back home to Franklin in the morning.

It had been a long, exciting, and *finally*, joyous day.

Blissful State

Lydia had recovered her strength by the time Douglas kissed her awake in mid-morning. He sat on her side of the bed and lifted her shoulders up to lean against his chest.

"Wake up sleepy-head. Are you going to sleep our honeymoon away?"

"No, I was trying to decide if I was awake or sleeping."

"What did you decide?"

"I'm still dreaming."

"I saw you turn over and smile, so I thought maybe you were waking up or I'd have let you sleep longer."

Without self-consciousness, she stretched her arms over her head and brought them down around Douglas' neck.

"I was awake, I didn't want to waste anymore of today sleeping. I wanted to wake up and be with you."

"I'm here. What do you want to do about it?"

"I can't say, or you might think I'm not very nice," she whispered into his ear, a bit afraid of what she was admitting. She held him tighter and hid her face in his shoulder.

"You are nice. You're wonderful and we'll do something about that right now." He gathered her into his arms and began to tease her awake with kisses down her neck, into the hollow of her throat and behind her ear. She shivered involuntarily.

"Where did you learn to do that?"

"I didn't have lessons, it comes naturally. I want to devour you with love all over, and we've got all summer. We're not going to hurry."

"Won't the other passengers on the boat think it's odd we

are staying in our cabin so late?"

"No, I went outside this morning and told the Captain you should rest today. He knows about your trip down the river, because he saw it. He's sorry that he had such a narrow gang-plank. He considers your fall his fault and has already remedied that. The whole crew is totally sympathetic with me taking care of you here. We won't be bothered, unless we want to be."

"I can get the Doctor if you wish. I'll get us breakfast after a bit and then we can rest or do whatever you want. This is a quiet part of the boat. The route to St. Louis isn't busy today. No one is to bother us, *Captain's orders.*"

"Let's stay in bed. Why don't you lay down beside me, so I can hug you. I'm sorry I went to sleep last night so early. I hope you weren't lonely. It wasn't the way I thought it would be."

"I wasn't lonely. I was thankful that you were sleeping peacefully with me and I still had you. I held you last night and you didn't awake. You cuddled closer and rested so quietly."

His voice was unsteady, "Oh, Lydia, you scared me so! I thought about Sarah when I couldn't reach you. It seemed I'd never catch up and you'd leave me." He held her so tightly she could hardly breath.

"It's all right, I'm fine," she soothed, as she stroked his hair. "I was afraid too. It was an accident and I've already learned to be more careful. I shouldn't have been so proud. We're here now and I'm fine."

"Hold onto me, Lydia."

"That's what I want to do. I'll never let you go, figuratively, if not literally."

Lydia returned Douglas' kisses. She breathed in his warmth, as she kissed the hollow of his throat. They lay in each other's arms, as they caressed and savored their new relationship. The soft morning light filtered through the window covering into their safe cocoon. *Their honeymoon shining, at last.*

It didn't matter where they were, they were in love and together at last, a fulfillment of their individual and collective dreams. The outcome was better than they'd imagined it could be, because they were in that state of bliss together.

⁓

My Ole Kentucky Home

They left the keel boat down river at Cairo, Illinois,
where the Mississippi and the Ohio Rivers merged. The happy
couple regained their land legs and their seats atop their horses,
marvelously rested and happy together. Their horses frisked,
relishing freedom as they moved over the fields of Kentucky.
They followed the Ohio River along the northern border of the
state toward Louisville. Lydia marveled as they moved along side
by side.

"I never felt so good. I guess I'll have to recommend a
bath in the Missouri after every wedding ceremony."

"Guess I'd have to go along with that, I went after you
and I feel wonderful too. Must be that Missouri River water."
They laughed and Douglas reached for Lydia's hand. They rode
on content.

Each night, they camped along the river, under their own
canvas or at inns along the way. They lazed along in weeks of
romantic odyssey. As they progressed into a warmer season, they
saw blooming trees and roses.

"In 1784, the adjoining states on the north issued a pact
giving Kentucky the northern shore of the Ohio River as their
boundary. Normally, each land division gets half a stream,"
Douglas commented as they rode along the Ohio's banks.

They left the Ohio River at Louisville to go through the
great horse country and found blue grass pastures.

The grass isn't blue until it blooms, but you can imagine
how it will look," Douglas explained.

The rolling hills resembled the green waves of a great ocean as the grass swayed in the breezes. These waves were capped with horse herds.

"Oh, look at the colts, they're racing already and they're just babies," Lydia de-lighted in the spindly-legged creatures.

At times, their own animals felt the urge to run and they allowed that freedom. The whole country made them feel alive, even the humans wished to run like the wind.

"When a foal is born, you can measure the leg from the hair of the hoof to the bend of the knee. Every one of those inches will become a hand of just over four inches each. That measurement will approximate the height of the horse as an adult," Douglas told her. "They call the male foals colts, and the females fillies."

"I know that, we do the same in Missouri, don't you remember?"

"Oh, I forgot you are a farm girl for a minute. Sorry."

Lydia continued his thought, "I can believe it. Look that little horse colt's legs come to where his mother's barrel attaches to her leg. His legs are as long, *almost* as hers!" Lydia marveled.

"Look how that younger black one looks like he's glued to his mother as they run. He hangs right under the mare's side. If they have their choice, they won't change their position. When he's a little older, he'll get braver and may run ahead of her. His dam is there if he gets frightened, he can always come back to her. When they wean these colts in September. They'll put some gentle old gelding or mare in the pasture with them. That gives the foals a friendly adult that won't spook so easily."

"It's amazing that his mommy doesn't step on him?"

"I think they do sometimes. It's surprising that you hardly ever see a crippled colt when they do all that running. Any you see lame are usually born crumpled up and some don't straighten out afterwards— I've seen them put splints, or boots, on their legs immediately after their birth."

"Does it really help?"

"I think it must, or they wouldn't continue to do it. The horses are so valuable here the veterinarians are some of the best in the world. It pays to raise healthy horses in this blue grass area of Kentucky. Fortunes and reputations are made on many a fine horse."

"What, no women raise horses?"

"I'm sorry, I meant *man* as a neutral term. There are some women who manage their own horse farms. I've seen some that ride better than men and have an eye for details. Come to think of it, they're lighter when in the saddle. I believe some of the women are better with foals than men. Maybe they speak more softly and move more gently."

"There are gentle men too. I'm sure you know my husband? There's no one gentler."

"Yes, I guess your husband is a gentle man."

"Aren't Kentucky-bred men supposed to be gentlemen?"

"Yes, but you know as well as I do that not *all* men *anywhere* can be gentlemen."

"You're right, the same goes for women, not all are ladies."

Lydia was quiet for a few miles.

"Douglas, don't take me wrong. Gentlemen are not sissies. My father isn't and you're certainly not."

A teasing light came into Douglas' eyes, if Lydia could have seen his face.

"Not what? A gentleman or sissy?"

"You are certainly a gentleman, and you certainly are *not* a sissy."

Douglas grinned and lifted her from her horse. He sat her across his lap in front of him and slowly smiled, then his head dipped to nuzzle her neck and kiss her. She giggled and smiled up into his face.

"What are you trying to do, show me that you aren't a gentleman?"

He placed his smiling lips on hers, looked into her face, then stopped his horse to allow her to clamber back aboard her own.

"Call me what you wish, I'm in love with you, Lady."

❧

They rode into Kentucky burley country where the natural limestone springs beneath the earth furnished the minerals in the soil.

"What's that building? I never saw so many black barns. I think they would be hot."

"That's a tobacco barn. See the cracks between the boards? That's to let the air circulate and the color is to make the barn hotter. They hang the tobacco leaves upside down in there to cure."

"There seems to be one on every farm."

"Yes, almost every farmer grows tobacco for a cash crop. You've seen plants in rows with those wide, rich leaves near Franklin. That's tobacco. When we were children, we used to have to go out and pick tobacco worms off the leaves."

"I've seen what we call tobacco worms in Missouri. Are they the same big nasty, green caterpillars we have?"

"Probably, they look about the same. You know how they leave just the stem on a plant? That's what they'd do to tobacco, if we didn't pick them off, one by one."

"I don't think I'd care much for that job."

"We didn't, but we made a game to see who could fill their bucket the fastest. The games made it go a little better. There was a whole field full of us sometimes including all the slave children. When all of us worked it didn't take long."

"Was it hot work?"

"Sultry. You swam in your own perspiration before long. We'd go down to the creek and take a dip when we finished. The slave boys and the white boys all went together and peeled off, buck naked."

"How did the girls cool off?"

"Who knows? I never bothered to think about it. They disappeared and I supposed they found other ways to cool off. When we got back to the house they were there, or around the cabins. We usually stayed in the creek for a couple of hours, they would have had time to do all sorts of things by the time we got there. They never liked it much that we went to the creek. If they got back to the house some of them had to work. We boys stayed away until most of the afternoon's work was done. I suppose we got a longer rest than the girls."

Douglas and Lydia were quiet for a few moments.

"Sometimes the boys put the tobacco worms on the girls, or ran after them like they were going to. The drover usually sent a grown person to oversee the children on our tobacco worm jobs. I expect he knew how we acted."

Douglas continued, "They were hard on us, if they checked our rows and found tobacco worms still on the leaves. We had to turn up every leaf and look at the underside. If the worm had been there for awhile, we could see the spines of the plant standing there all bare, otherwise, maybe just a few missing bites around the edges. We had to look very closely, because if we missed some tobacco worms, evidence of their scourge soon showed up and they'd make us do the field again. We didn't like to spend anymore time there than we had to. It was too hot out."

"The limestone spring water from the hills is used to turn Kentucky's corn into
whiskey. Lydia, I suppose you can guess what Bourbon County is named after?"

"No—o—oo, I'd never be able to guess that," Lydia answered facetiously. Her mood changed, "Why are there so many slaves through here?"

"Tobacco and cotton require hand labor. That's why the slaves are considered necessary to Kentucky's livelihood."

"I preferred the horses in that blue grass country. At least the slaves there looked as if they were enjoying themselves. That little brown jockey was about the best *burr* I've ever seen stuck to a horse. He was dwarfed. I would have been afraid to ride that fast, but he liked it."

"The owners keep the weight down so they can win, especially when they gamble on the races. The horse with a lighter weight in the saddle lasts longer than one weighed down by a full-size man. *Keep everything light, the saddle, bridle, and the rider*, is their motto."

Lydia noticed that Douglas began to look ahead and didn't linger so long looking at the sights. "Are you anxious to get home?"

"Yes, tomorrow, we'll be where I grew up. It's just a few miles further."

"In a way, I'll be sorry when we get there," Lydia sighed. "I've enjoyed our time together, just the two of us." She reached for Douglas' hand. He squeezed hers in return. He leaned from his horse to give her a quick kiss.

"Have you noticed how our horses walk close together to help us out? I think they know how much we love each other," Douglas said.

"They like each other too, but they're not always fond of this mule tagging along. He sometimes gets impatient and pinches them, then they aim a kick at him in return, but they're a peaceful lot in general. Can we ride when we get to your old home?"

"Yes, we'll leave the mule in the barn while we're here. Thank goodness, I'm tired of dragging him along everywhere we go. I want to show you the plantation and the best way for us to do that is to ride out in the morning or evening while it's cool. We'll visit around with the family some and give these horses a rest too. When we go back to Missouri, we'll take a side-wheeler to St. Louis and won't ride horseback so many miles. By then we'll be anxious to get home and back to school by the end of summer."

"Don't hurry the summer too much. You sound eager to go home already and I haven't met anyone yet," Lydia added.

They rode along in companionable silence for a few more miles. Evening was advancing when they stopped near Lexington for supper and a bed at an inn. Douglas went to sleep early, but Lydia lay awake wondering about tomorrow's happenings.

Douglas is wonderful, but I miss my family already. Will I be the one most eager to go home at the end of the summer? Mother always says to make the best of things, I resolve to do so. I hope they like me— and I, them. Dear Lord, help me through tomorrow. Be with my family at home. You know about everyone of us. Take care of us in all that we do that it might be after your will. Thank you for keeping us safe. Your will be done tomorrow- and always. Amen.

Lydia turned her pillow over for a cool spot, but she didn't soon sleep in the sultry dark of their room.

The In-Laws, in The Valley

They rode through beautiful verdant country. Lydia's stomach tightened in anticipation. She was about to meet her new in-laws for the first time, and see Douglas' ancestral home.

"Close your eyes, I'll tell you when to open them," Douglas directed as he reined his horse on the shaded gravel road.

Lydia obeyed, even though she didn't want to miss a moment. She grabbed Douglas' arm to keep herself steady. H After they rounded the bend in the road, he caught the reins of her horse and stopped both animals. The pack mule took advantage of the stop and cocked his hip to rest. Douglas patted Lydia's hand and reached to kiss her on the cheek.

"Let me have one more moment alone with you before I have to share you." He turned her face with his hand, kissed her gently on the lips.

"Lydia, you're beautiful."

She lifted her face and smiled with her eyes closed.

"You can look now."

Lydia opened her eyes to look questioningly into his face, then turned her head to the front. She gave a quick intake of breath.

"Oh-h, you must be— rich? The house is beautiful, but it's huge."

"Yes, it is huge and lovely. I grew up here, but I haven't been back for almost three years."

"They may think I married you for your money."

"How could they think that, you didn't know I had any?"

"Yes, but maybe they don't know that. Why *did* you leave— and teach, when you could have stayed here and lived well?"

"I was *called* to teach, I couldn't do anything else and please God, then I needed to leave Kentucky because of that divorce. My brother Rob liked the plantation. I didn't abandon them, I left it in good hands. He and my father run it the way they want. I purposely haven't taken money. I wanted to make it on my own and I'm happy with what I'm doing and who I married."

"I love who I married."

"So that's that. Mrs. Charlton, let's go meet your new family."

Inside Lydia quivered. *This scares me more than anything I've ever done. Why do I feel so—inadequate and childish all of a sudden?* She looked at her rumpled riding habit.

"I wish I had put on a dress and we'd rented a buggy. I feel kind of— *out of place.*"

"I'm sorry, we could have done that. I didn't think. It's faster on horseback. I was getting anxious to get home, show you off, and see my family again."

Douglas guided his horse into the circular drive in front of the huge white columns. Lydia quietly followed. A dignified slave in purple livery came to hold the head of Douglas' horse. Without direction, another slave appeared and led Lydia's horse to a mounting block for her to alight. She stepped off and straightened her skirts.

"Marsh Douglas I'm glad you home, I didn't know you! You ain't been home for so long."

"Thank you Willie, you're the first to see us. This is my wife, Lydia Williams Charlton. Lydia, Willie has been with us since before I was born, he's in charge of the stables here on Fairbank, the home plantation. His wife Tilde cooks in the kitchen and his son, Marcus takes care of the stables at The Valley. The whole family lives close."

"I'm pleased to meet you, Willie. I'm glad your family lives close. I love my family and I'd hate to be away from them." Lydia thought, *I put my foot in that. Why did I mention the*

family being close by or that I'd hate to be away from mine.
They'll think I'm referring to slave families and I don't want to
come visit Douglas' home. I don't know if their family is all
here. Homesick baby, watch your speech.

"Where is everyone, Willie? It seems kind of quiet around here," Douglas asked.

"They's over at The Valley getting rooms ready so you newlyweds can have your privacy. You got here early, they ain't 'pectin' you so soon. They's planned a big party for Saturday night." He covered his mouth, "Uh-huh, they may wantons surprise you. Don't tell 'em I told you. Go on in, Telltale fix you some 'freshens while you wait. They's ought be home anytime now."

Lydia took Douglas' arm to step from the block. They turned toward the steps to the wide verandah and the double front doors of the mansion.

"Hurry, I'll have time to get washed and get into a dress. It will make me feel more presentable."

"Bring our satchels to my old room and send one of the girls with bath water as soon as you can," Douglas directed a young male slave who appeared on the verandah. "We'll wait for refreshments 'til after we get dressed, if there's time before the family arrives."

Lydia had plenty of time to dress to her satisfaction. Actually she had so much time, that she grew nervous all over again. Tilde had served them some kind of fruit juice and now her stomach felt queasy. Her insides fluttered as they waited in the parlor. *Take a deep breath and think of something else.* She rose for the third time and walked across the rich carpet in front of the elaborate marble mantel ornamenting the fireplace.

"What's the matter, Honey? Are you nervous? You don't need to be, it's just family."

"I know, but they're not my family— until I get to know them. I hope they like me."

"They are your family. You're married to me, aren't you?"
"Yes."

"Automatically when you married me, you got them. Like it or not, that's the way it works, don't you remember?" Douglas attempted to lighten the moment. "Don't forget I chose you, you're the most beautiful woman I ever saw, I love you and you're *my wife.*"

"Oh, Douglas, you're good for me. I should straighten up, but it's hard. I keep imagining the worst."

Douglas took her into his arms. He steadied her by rubbing up and down her back.

"That makes me feel — "

There was a noise in the hallway and a woman's voice spoke out.

"Well here's the newlyweds. You got here before we expected you, but welcome, welcome."

Guiltily, Lydia stepped away from Douglas.

Douglas reached out an arm, encircled her waist, drew her back against his side.

"Mother, I'd like you to meet my wife. This is Lydia Williams Charlton, whom I love dearly. Lydia, my mother, Elizabeth Sidwell Charlton. I hope you'll become good friends."

Mrs. Charlton looked closely at Lydia and then put out her hand. Lydia reached for it tentatively and Mrs. Charlton drew her into a brief embrace, kissing the air on both sides of Lydia's cheeks. She stepped back to survey Lydia more fully.

"We're pleased to have you visit us. We haven't seen Douglas for nearly three years and we could hardly wait for him to get home." She returned to the business of hosting, "Did you find what you needed in your room? We weren't expecting you until Friday, or Saturday, but you can stay here until later in the week when the house is ready at The Valley. We're having a reception on Saturday evening for the neighbor-ing planters. They all want to see Douglas after all this time— and meet his *new bride.*"

♠

The couple were moved to the house at The Valley as soon as the party was over. Lydia's head swam with all the names, places and things she had to learn about her family in

Kentucky.

*I'm happy to be alone with Douglas after this past week,
but I feel kind of like— they didn't want me at Fairbank. Am I an
embarrassment to them?*

The *people* on the plantations weren't accustomed to a
lady riding over the plantation with the men.

Lydia overheard female slaves speak to one another. "It
ain't fit in' for a lady to sashay around with the men. Just look at
her ricin' where she ain't wanted. It ain't decent."

*Douglas wants to show me all of his boyhood haunts, I
wonder if the whole plantation thinks I'm out of my place. I
wanted to see everything, but now, I feel embarrassed to
accompany Douglas. My home in Missouri is a slave state.
Where we live has just over one quarter colored. Southern atti-
tudes are reflected along the rivers there. Despite this, I'm not
prepared for the plantation system here. It's immense, so
different from home. My family doesn't have slaves, even though
some of our neighbors do. Help me Lord to understand this.
Douglas falls so easily into command of these people. What does
he really think— feel about them?*

"Don't you want to go with me? I want to show you the
cotton gin," Douglas begged. "It
takes a slave a whole day to clean a pound. Have you ever tried to
take the seeds out of cotton? It's hard." Lydia hung back. "I'll
show you when we get to the gin. I want you to see.
Come on."

She gave in and went along, but felt ill at ease knowing
the feeling of the people on the plantation.

"You're awfully quiet, Honey, do you feel well?" Douglas
questioned. Her mood troubled him. "What's the matter? Is the
heat too much for you?"

Finally, she told him. "The slaves don't think it's right for
a lady to ride out among the field hands. I get the impression your
mother thinks the same thing. I don't want to do anything to upset
your family. Because I'm from Missouri, I don't want them to

think I'm backward or don't know my way around. I'll do whatever I need to, to get along and seem proper to you."

"We don't live here. It doesn't matter what the slaves
think. I'll talk to Mother and we'll straighten this thing out. I want
you with me, so I can show you things we've talked about from
my childhood."

"Please don't mention it to your mother. I don't want her
to think I'm a tattler. I can stay in the house and do what ladies
do. That's fine."

"We'll see, but I want you with me. We share when we're
out in the fields alone. It's our best time here and I'm not giving it
up. Lydia, I love you, don't ever forget that, no matter what
anyone says or does here, or anywhere else."

⌐⇔⌐

Plantation Life

"Douglas, I didn't intend to snoop, but it has become obvious to me every morning when we go outside. Did you know the overseer stays in one of the slave women's cabin at night?"

"Yes, the family knows. Mr. Seats and Liza have been as good as married for about ten years."

"Do her children belong to him?"

"I imagine. I'd never thought to question it."

"Their children work in the yard with the other slave children. He doesn't pay any special attention to them, at least not during the day when I'm outside with them. Why don't they get married, if everyone here seems to know they are together as a couple?"

"It just isn't done, whites *marrying* slaves."

"People here seem so— *separate and callous.*"

"Color means much here, most places. I think it's been that way throughout history. Just look at the Old Testament. Ishmael and Isaac were not of the same race— at least on their mother's side. Their family groups still dislike each other. There have been slaves of all races throughout history.

There can be prejudice both ways. I read somewhere that the white slaves from the area that became the British Isles made poor slaves in the estimation of peoples from the middle east. Some of the biggest slave dealers in Africa were in league with conquering Chieftains selling their own race, maybe even their own tribal members."

"It seems that a person's standing depends mostly on color here."

"I'm afraid that's right, except for the poor whites up in the hills. The slaves are the only ones considered lower."

"I never thought much about slavery one way or the other before we came here," Lydia remarked.

"It's present at Boonville and Franklin, even next door to your parents."

"I know, but I wasn't involved one way or the other before."

"It's here, we can't change the institution overnight. I think some time in the future, slavery will gradually diminish and fade away, but not tomorrow or next year, or even in ten years. I don't know, but that's my opinion. Slave trade is being frowned on by some countries now."

"I'm glad. I don't like it!"

"Don't speak too loudly around the plantations or you'll have us tarred and feathered. It will soon be time to go home again, let's get along with the family for the short time we'll be here."

"*Out of sight, out of mind?* I don't think so, I won't be able to forget this even when I'm away from it and I'm going to look at slaves at home differently too. I'll not take them for granted so easily again. I've gotten to know Willie, Tilde, and Marcus, they're no different than you or I."

"The whites around here, would say that's *near blasphemy*."

"Well it isn't and I'm willing to tell them so."

Mrs. Charlton overheard the conversation and was thoroughly unsettled by Lydia's attitude, however she let Douglas' attitude pass over her head without notice. *Blood is thicker than water* and a mother often overlooks those things in her own child she considers faults in another. Lydia's attitude toward slavery added another black mark to Mrs. Charlton's tally of the girl's faults.

Lydia saw little of Douglas' father. He came into the house only long enough to sleep and eat. The balance of his time was taken up with the summer's work on the plantations. He was out from dawn to dusk, and with the long summer days, those were very long hours away from home.

Lydia saw Rob only in passing at social events used to introduce her as Douglas' bride. Rob was distant, preoccupied with running a plantation and courting a belle two counties away. He prepared The Valley Plantation house for their home and didn't linger long at Fairbank, except during harvest time.

ﾝﾑ

In the afternoon, as Lydia walked down the stairs, she heard a distant scream. She ran to the window on the landing and looked outside. All she could see was dust coming down the road at a fast pace. She tripped on down the stairs and out the front door to the verandah. The dust was nearing and she could see the small horse lunging as it ran with the light dog cart whipping dangerously from side to side.

Mrs. Charlton took out the dog cart to go to The Valley today! Her horse is out of control, the dog cart is going to turn over. I can't see her inside, maybe she fell out.

Lydia raced to the circle drive and crowded the horse into the hedge. He veered away from her waving arms. Wild-eyed, he caught the cart wheels in the hedge, bringing himself and the cart to an abrupt halt. Lydia reached for his head.

In terror, Raven reared and struck out with his front feet. Accustomed to horses, Lydia stepped around his feet and bore into his shoulder, caught the check rein and pulled. The pressure turned his head into the shrubbery. He settled and stood shaking. She spoke to him in a softer voice as she moved her hand up his shoulder and grasped the lines just behind the bit.

"It's all right, it's all right. Take it easy. You're going to be fine."

He calmed and shook his head, slinging foam. She put forward pressure on the bit, and he stepped from the hedge onto the smoothly raked driveway He stood shakily with his legs splayed weakly under him. Willie appeared from the direction of the barn.

"Miss Lydia, what you do to Raven? He's lathered from head to hoof!"

"I don't know Willie, he came in running and I managed to crowd him into the hedge and get hold of the rein. Mrs. Charlton took him out about two hours ago and this is the first I've seen of him. We'd better get out and start looking for Mrs. Charlton, she may be hurt."

The pair heard a noise.

"Ooh— Lydia, I'm here. In the cart. He threw me down when a bird flew up right under his nose. I can't get up. Help me."

"Willie, here, you hold Raven and I'll see what she needs."

Lydia went to the rear of the dogcart. She looked in to find an array of skirts and a body moving under the petticoats. She reached in and starting pulling the skirts down over the protruding feet. Finally she reached Mrs. Charlton to find her face scrapped raw down one side, but pale and hot on the other side.

"Does anything hurt more than the rest, Mrs. Charlton?"

"No, I feel better with my skirt out of my face. At least I can breath now."

"I'll go get Tilde and a cold wet cloth, maybe by then, if you don't have anything else hurting you, we can get you out of there."

Lydia stepped to Willie's side.

"I'll get Tilde, you hold Raven here in the shade and we'll be right out. I'll get some
others to help too, so we can lift Mrs. Charlton."

Lydia ran around the house to the kitchen.

"Tilde, Mrs. Charlton has had a runaway, she thinks she's not hurt, but we need help to get her out of the cart. Bring water and a cool cloth."

Tilde grabbed the water bucket and clean hand towels from the back porch and headed through the house, yelling as she went, with Lydia in her wake.

"Bessie, Lige get yourselves down and in front. We need help!"

Tilde was in control now, everyone moved to her directions.

Lydia dipped a hand towel in the water bucket and wrung out the excess water. She stepped up into the dog cart and bathed Mrs. Charlton's face.

"Lydia, I want to sit up now, will you give me your hand?"

Lydia grasped Mrs. Charlton's hand and put her other arm behind her mother in law's shoulders. Gently she eased Mrs. Charlton to a sitting position. Mrs. Charlton groaned and lowered her head between her knees.

"I feel faint— let me sit here a minute"

"Just take your time, we're in no rush."

Tears rolled down Mrs. Charlton's cheeks. Lydia had never seen her look so vulnerable. Lydia kept her arm around the older woman's shoulders and patted her. The woman turned her face to Lydia's shoulder and muffled her tears and her voice.

"Lydia— I'm embarrassed. I'm glad that you didn't let Willie see me laying here with my skirts over my head. Thank you."

"Don't worry about appearances now, we all want you to be well. Everyone here loves you."

After a few more minutes, Mrs. Charlton nodded that she was ready to try to get out of the dogcart.

Lydia turned her head and spoke, "Lige, will you bring the mounting box and come here please?"

Lydia stood up and helped Mrs. Charlton to her feet, where she swayed, but straightened her spine and attempted to present her usual strong appearance to the slaves.

Lige placed the box under the rear of the dogcart and reached his hand up in support. Lydia kept hold of Mrs. Charlton, her arm around the older woman's waist and lifting as she assisted her in her descent. The big slave gently lowered Mrs. Charlton to the box, where her left leg gave way beneath her, she fell against him. Lydia braced herself in time to prevent both of them from spilling down Lige. He eased his mistress to the driveway, kept hold of her with one arm, then reached for Lydia to assist her descent.

On the driveway, Lydia put her shoulder under Mrs. Charlton's arm and Tilde placed herself in a like position on the other side. The trio limped to the porch.

"Bessie, why don't you go fix Mrs. Charlton's bed and we'll get her inside. Thank you Lige and Willie. I think we ladies can make it now," Lydia said.

Mrs. Charlton sat down in the rocker when she got up the steps to the verandah. She lay her head back on the chair, closed her eyes. Tilde hurried to the kitchen for the smelling salts and Lydia knelt at her mother in law's feet and pushed the hair back out of Mrs. Charlton's face. She plucked a fan from the adjoining chair and fanned the flushed lady.

The reclining lady opened her eyes and looked into Lydia's face. Her own face softened.

"Lydia, you risked your life for me. I see why Douglas loves you. I haven't been fair to you. Now, I accept Douglas' judgment of your character. We were all so wrong on Sallie, I let that influence me. You've been nothing but
kind to me and I'm sorry for the way I've acted."

Lydia was uncomfortable with Mrs. Charlton's frankness.

"That's fine, we needed to get acquainted and it's taken us a little longer maybe, but we'll make it. I love Douglas and you do too. I know you want the best for him, just as I would, if he were my own son."

"No, let me finish, you are his chosen one and I'm proud and pleased in his choice. I hope you'll grow to accept our way of life when you better understand it."

Lydia left, *Not likely* unspoken and intently looked into Mrs. Charlton's face.

"I do love Douglas. I mean to make him the happiest I can. Isn't that what really matters to you?"

"Yes, dear, it is."

"I doubt if I will ever totally understand plantation life, but. . ."

"No, dear, don't say anything. I can't tell anyone and I don't let on, but I don't like slavery either. I have to live with it, so I make the best of it, just as you'll make the best of what you can't change in your own life."

"I— never guessed"

"It's our little secret dear. Now, I think I'm ready to go to my bedroom, if you'll help me again."

Mrs. Charlton rested that day and was fully recovered back to her normal self by the third day. Rice powder covered her raw cheek.

The next day, she drew Lydia aside to speak privately with her.

"Please forgive me for the way I've acted. I've been ashamed of myself, but couldn't seem to stop. We love Douglas so and we've been afraid for him to be away from us so long."

Lydia soothed, "Douglas has managed to endear himself to the people of Boonville and Franklin. He's taught a group of men to read and he's wonderful at the Academies. He was my instructor and never let on to anyone that he was interested in me until I told him that I wasn't going to go back. I lost a dear friend and I couldn't be there any longer. Douglas had asked my parents almost a year before if he could see me, but he waited patiently until they thought I was ready before he spoke a word to me. I think you have much to be proud of as to his conduct away from his family. He's been a true gentleman and a fine Christian man." Lydia's love made her brave in her defense of Douglas.

Mrs. Charlton was aware of Lydia's love and courage for the first time.

"Thank you for telling me this, you didn't have to."

"I wanted to tell you, because I'm so proud of Douglas and you should be too."

"Believe me, Dear, I am. Lydia, I never had a grown daughter, but if I had, I'd have wanted her to be like you. I can see you love Douglas, you'll help him be an even stronger man, and I can see you make him happy."

꒰ꕤ

The duration of the newlywed's stay was uneventful, but Lydia breathed a sigh of relief when they boarded a flat-bottomed sternwheeler on the Ohio River at the end of the next week.

Douglas patted her hand as they stood at the rail waving their farewells to the family gathered on the dock.

"I'm proud of you. You and Mother seemed to get along better after Raven ran away with her. I know she's a little overbearing at times, but we probably won't be back for a few years. By that time they'll forgive us our views on slavery and it will be a closed subject. *If* we happen to bring them a grandchild, all will be *forgiven, forever.*"

"Douglas, it's not something to joke about. I do get along better with your mother. I hope we made some progress. I didn't see enough of your father to get to know him. Maybe another time, if they'd come to Missouri, we'd keep them away from work a little while, then we'd have time to sit down and really talk with him and your brother Rob."

Baby Rabbits, Corncob Dolls and a Slave Child

When Lydia and Douglas prepared to land on the docks at St. Charles, Missouri, they saw a pair of scruffy men at the end of the gangplank. Realization of their intention hit Lydia.

"Douglas, those men are trying to sell that little Negro slave child to the first class passengers leaving this steamer."

The older man sneered, "Lady, don't you need a little lap dog? Buy this pretty little pickaninny and have your own little pet."

"Right here, lady, she's a bargain."

"She's gonna be high yellar; worth thousands. Get her young, train her your way."

Some looked speculatively, but most turned aside and ignored the men.

"Too many years before she'd be productive," answered one finely dressed man.

The handsome couple awaited their turn to walk, carefully down the landing ramp. From the shade of the pilot cabin, Lydia heard the remarks and saw the child. She turned to whisper to Douglas, as they neared.

"Oh, Douglas that poor child. They're selling her. Let's buy her and get her out of this mess. She's so dirty and they look— *evil*," Lydia shuddered involuntarily. "They don't care anything about her feelings. Just look at the way they shove her forward so roughly."

Douglas stepped in front of Lydia, turned his back to the ramp and spoke softly.

"You go on down the dock after we get on firm footing. Let me bargain with them. If they see that you want the child, they'll be more reluctant to sell for a reasonable price, or hold out on selling her hoping to generate more interest. Keep walking."

Lydia and Douglas looked away from the fate of the child, as they walked down the planks. Lydia walked a half a block away and turned to look back as Douglas returned to the men where they shouted the child's attributes to the final passengers leaving the steamer.

As Lydia stood alone, an elaborately dressed man, rode by in a carriage. He tapped its roof with his cane. The driver slowed.

"Stop here, I want out," he ordered.

The driver pulled the carriage over and hauled back on the reins of the splendid bay team. The flashily dressed man alighted and walked back toward Lydia.

He paraded near the young woman but failed to draw her attention. He walked closer, her worried attention remained down the docks.

Turning aside for a moment, he drew a long slim, ornately beribboned package from his inside coat pocket. He glanced back over his shoulder to find her attention still focused further down the dock. He came up behind Lydia, walked very close to her back and bent over. As he came up with the wrapped package in his hand, he spoke.

"Excuse me, Ma'am, I think you dropped this parcel."

Lydia turned distractedly to the man.

"What, what was that?" She didn't change the direction of her gaze.

"I think you dropped your parcel.

She barely glanced at the package.

"No. No, it's not mine."

She looked back to where Douglas was dickering with the scruffy men over the child.

"It must be yours, it was right here behind you. You would have noticed it, had you stepped over it before."

"No, it isn't mine."

"A beautiful lady standing here alone, it isn't safe, may I escort you?"

"I'm not alone, I'm waiting for someone."

"But you seem to be deserted. My carriage is at the curb,

I'd be happy to take you and your parcels anywhere you'd like to go."

"No, I'm fine." She still didn't focus on him. Lydia's beauty and reaction presented a challenge.

"But, surely you are alone. As you can see, there is no one standing about," he persisted, as he drew nearer to her face.

Lydia looked full into the face of the man for the first time. She saw an unusually handsome man, by many standards. A cynical twist on his smiling mouth and a look in his eyes that she didn't understand gave her an inward flutter of alarm.

"I'm fine," she turned and took two steps away.

He caught her arm. "I insist that I escort you."

She attempted to disengage his hand from her upper arm, pulled and he grasped more tightly.

A voice rang out as the tug of war escalated.

"That teams running away! Sir, sir, is that your carriage?"

The man turned and looked for his carriage, it was not in sight.

"Where, where did it go?"

"Around the corner, they were running and the driver was unable to control them. Hurry, you may be able to catch up before they get far."

The man took off in the direction Douglas pointed.

Douglas grabbed Lydia's arm, whirled her about and steered to the little girl standing alone on the dock.

"I've got her, let's get out of here."

He scooped the bedraggled little girl into his other arm as she clutched her tiny bundle. The couple walked quickly away from the docks in the opposite direction of the *runaway* carriage. The little girl buried her face in her bundle and snuffled.

"Let's hurry, he doesn't know that his team didn't run away. By the time he catches up with them, we'll be gone," Douglas whispered.

On the way to the inn, Lydia commented to Douglas.

"Oh, Douglas, I'm so glad you were- *successful*. Poor little thing. Just look at all this dirt. There hasn't been a bath in a long while. Let's go to the inn and get everything cleaned up. I can put her in some of our clean clothes and we can send someone from the inn to get some things. I don't want to take these rags home. Let's have the maid burn them."

The little girl kept her face buried in her bundle.

After their care, the child clutched a corncob doll, the only item from her bundle to which she gave special interest. The doll had scraps of cloth for clothes. She fell asleep in their big iron bed.

The couple awaited the return of the maid with a child's wardrobe.

"I don't know what possessed that man on the dock."

"Sweetheart, don't you know? Men like that prey upon beautiful or innocent young women they think are helpless or alone. He thought he had an easy mark when he saw you standing there," Douglas laughed.

"What are you laughing at?"

"Had I waited a little longer, I have a feeling that you would have shown him that you weren't so defenseless. You didn't grow up with your brothers not learning a little about self protection. I've seen that in our play. You might have given him worse than I could have." Now it was amusing for both.

"How did you know I was having trouble with him? The last time I looked, you were very busy with those two men."

"The two left after they got their money and signed the bill of sale. I turned to signal you that I had her and saw a man hanging on to your arm. I told Addie to stand still. She was so scared, she froze. I started over. If he didn't unhand you and I knocked his arm away, I knew there would be an altercation, and *now* I have *two ladies* to consider. I decided to use my brain and save all of us from possible injury. The dock hands made the drivers move their carriages. I simply took that advantage to avoid a fight, and here we all three are, safe and sound."

"That *gentleman* is on a wild goose chase and I hope we never see him again." Lydia rose, to look at the cherub in their bed. She brushed a soft ash-blonde curl from the forehead and bent closer.

"The men I got her from, said her name was Addie. But

the name is Ruth Curry, on the bill of sale. They said they knew nothing else about her, other than the information written on the papers."

"She's beautiful. Did you notice that she's lighter than she was before? I guess all that dirt made her look brown."

"Many slaves are mixed. Mulattos, it's hard to tell who their parents are on some plantations. Didn't you notice before?"

"Yes, but I could tell that they were part Negro. There are features that give away the secret, even when they are very light. This child doesn't have any of those features."

"Some of the babies don't show their *coloured* blood until they're older, than usually some characteristics show."

"It doesn't matter to me if she does or doesn't look *colored*. Poor little thing. I never saw such a dirty and bedraggled little child as when we first saw her. She looked so abandoned. With her big teary, blue eyes, she was like a frightened baby rabbit frozen before a snake. We'll never let that happen to her again, no matter what happens to us. I love you Douglas for rescuing poor Addie from those men. Thank you."

"Is that the only reason you love me?"

"No, of course not, but you already know that." She reached to squeeze his hand and he pulled her into his arms.

"One last kiss, then we've got to get some rest. We have an early morning if we want to get well on our way to Franklin tomorrow. This little tyke may not be able to ride as far as we can in a day."

The pair lay in the big iron bed, on either side of the child. They nestled her between them. Several times during the night, she cried out; both drew her into their arms, comforted her; drew her close to their bodies and hearts. She was exhausted and didn't completely awaken, but clung to them, seeming to be extremely frightened, even in sleep.

♮

August 1826
<u>Franklin</u>?

"Let's ride the Boone's Lick Trail. It's a good road on the north side of the Missouri River. I've traveled it before and it will give us time to get acquainted with our new daughter," suggested Douglas.

"That's fine with me, we haven't had enough time together for a long while. I've had to share you with your family and fellow travelers. It will be nice to be together in our own little family again."

Addie was opening up with them. She now talked and Lydia could tell she was bright by the way she looked at things. They practiced talking as they rode along. When they came to towns, or to other people, Addie immediately became shy again. At times, she hid her face in Lydia's or Douglas' shoulder and wouldn't look at others.

"Look Douglas and Addie, at that cedar on top of the bluff. It looks like a needle with hair," Lydia laughingly pointed to the cedar.

"That's cedar pyramid. I read about it somewhere. Not too far from here on the other bank, there's supposed to be a big cave where settlers used to take shelter. If we were on the other side, we could sleep there tonight."

"Oh, Papa, we can't twim across the riber. We'd get drownded."

"You're right. Your mommy tried it once and we both got wet. Ask her about swallowing river water."

"The swallowing wasn't so bad, it was breathing that was the problem."

Addie never tired of hearing of their adventures, "Before I was your liddle girl."

The trio rode into a little river town where the town dogs and dirty little children, *brown and white*, ran along beside their horses and the mule. Addie became particularly frightened and hid in Douglas' arms. They quickly found a tavern and secured a room. Lydia carried the quietly snuffling Addie up behind the maid, as Douglas finished their arrangements.

"That kid ain't goin' cry all night, is she?"

"No, she's just frightened now. She'll be fine. Usually she's very quiet. Would you have someone bring up warm water and what's on your menu for our supper. We're tired and won't come back down tonight. Here's payment for our breakfast too and we'll be on our way shortly after first light, so we'd appreciate an early meal. Thank you."

Addie fearfully watched the brown servant, as she set down the tray with the trio's supper. Lydia and Douglas were unable to understand her feelings.

"You's put the tray outside when you's finish. I'll pick it up."

"Thank you, that's fine. Here's something for you." Douglas handed the maid several coins. She looked surprised and curtsied.

"Oh— thank you, Suh."

After the close of their meal. Addie slept in the big bed. Lydia and Douglas discussed their day.

"Douglas, do you think it's because she's been a slave that she hides from people?"

"That's a possibility. She had a strange reaction to the children this afternoon and to the maid tonight. I don't understand, but colored people aren't treated real well in Missouri or Kentucky. That may be why she is so shy. Lydia, I think she's coming out of it a little, don't you?"

"She doesn't look coloured and we treat her like our own daughter. I don't see how a stranger could even imagine her as a slave."

"I don't think they do, but in her mind she may feel that way or she's had some bad experiences, somewhere, somehow—."

"I hope she soon forgets that part of her life." Lydia was

thoughtful, "Where are we going to tell people we got her when we get to Franklin and Boonville?"

"I don't know Lydia. That's a hard one. I've always been honest and told the truth. Can't we just do that?"

"No, I don't want them to know we bought her. I just want her to be ours and that's that."

"I've been gone from Kentucky nearly four years. What if they think she's my own child?" Douglas questioned.

"Oh, I hadn't thought of that! People that know you, won't think that."

"Yes, but people have to have some explanation or they'll *make* one up."

"Can't we just tell them she's an orphan and we adopted her?" Lydia asked.

"Yes, I think we had better, but that may not stop speculation."

"Let's tell them we got her at St. Charles. They all know that wasn't your home. I expect the rest will get the message soon enough with the grapevine we've got in Boonville and Franklin."

"That's fine with me. Maybe they'll soon forget that we brought her back with us and accept her for who she is now," Douglas said.

"I hope so. We've *got to make it happen*."

୧ଈ

The week passed.

Ever the teacher, Douglas expounded to Addie and Lydia as they rode along. They passed a bluff with rocks in the shape of a huge face in its heights.

"Look Addie, do you see the face in the rocks? The Indians thought that was a sign for the Great Spirit. We call him God and they called this stream of water Monitou after their name for God. The early settlers changed the Indian name to Moniteau. This stream is named Moniteau after the face on the rock. The bigger stream is called the Missouri River. That's the one Mommy fell into and I had to pull her out. We need to be careful around water, we don't want you to fall in."

Lydia pointed, "Oh Addie and Douglas, look at the red paintings on the rocks."

"We were talking about Indians before. They painted those a long time ago. There's a buffalo, a deer and what's that other animal?"

"Doggie," Addie spoke with great assurance.

"It might be a dog. It looks like the animals you draw on my writing paper," Douglas said.

The trio rode on, exclaiming over the sights.

"We're close to Rocheport. Look back to the south, the bluffs must be over a hundred and fifty feet high. Those sure would be hard to climb," Douglas commented.

"Addie, Look down here, the trees and the river look small from up here."

"Rocheport means rock port or the French insisted it be called Port of Rocks. Boats stop at ports, but usually a port is on a big, big body of water. We stopped at some landings, that's the same thing. It's a place where we can tie up a boat. Some of the places are little and some are big, just like some of the boats are little, and some big."

"Douglas, we're getting close to home, aren't we?"

"We have the twenty mile prairie, *Spanish Needle Prairie*, I guess for all those yellow flowers that grow there," Douglas commented.

"You mean we found something that you don't know for sure?"

"Am I being too much the professor?"

"No, I like for you to explain things to us. Sometimes you even hit on something I don't already know."

"Sorry. I'll tell you something you do want to hear. After we cross this prairie, we'll be almost there."

Addie looked into Lydian's face. "Will my other mommy be home when we get there?"

"No, baby, she's gone, but we're here with you. Were you with your other mommy when she died?"

"Yes, she sick. Sometimes wake up coughin'."

"Do you know what was wrong with her?"

"A man with a black bag comed. He said new-mom-ah."

"Pneumonia?" Addie nodded. "Did he come often?"

"No, don't 'member him again."

"Then what happened?"

"She in bed all day, I get her drink, she all red. She bleeded."

"From where? Her mouth?"

"Nose."

"Oh, she had a nose bleed?

"Yes, she sleep and sleep. I couldn't wake her up. I cry. Men's come and take me. I didn't see Mommy nomore."

"Do you know when that was? Were you with the men one day, two days, or long time?"

"One night, then till I hungry next day. They hurted my arm rubbing on black stuff. Then I see Papa. He take me to you. I get *new mommy,* like Papa say." Addie crowded closer and closer to Lydia as she talked. Lydia wrapped her arms securely around the little girl and rocked with her face buried in the child's hair to hide her own tears.

"I'm glad you weren't alone long. You were just waiting to be our little girl and now
everything is fine. We love you and we're your mommy and papa."

"I lub you."

"We can tell you do. You hug and kiss us and we're very happy that you belong to us and we belong to you. We're a family."

"I kiss my other mommy too."

"Sure you did. You loved her too." Lydia looked over Addie's curly head to Douglas' eyes. Tears washed down her cheeks.

Douglas reached out and wiped her cheek with his palm. He mouthed, "I love you both."

They spent one more night on the prairie, too tired to ride into the darkness. Lydia slept fitfully and arose earlier than usual. She watched the blaze of sunrise over the hills. Then got on her knees to nuzzle Douglas' neck.

He spoke quietly, "I was waiting for you."

"No, you were asleep, I looked."

"You just thought I was. I watched the sun light your

face." He looked very serious. "Do you know you glow?"

"Silly."

"No, seriously, Lydia, you do glow, but you don't need the sun."

"Douglas, there must be light to see anyone's face."

"I can see you even in the dark." He reached for her face and moved his hand up her cheek, then pulled her close to him. She lay beside him.

"We'll be back with family again tonight. This is our last day on our own for awhile."

"Douglas, I'm scared."

"Why?"

"We've been so happy together."

He pulled her into the security of his arms.

"Don't worry. No one can separate us, we only have ourselves to contend with."

Snuggling comfortably, Lydia fell back to sleep.

Douglas lay awake with her head on his shoulder and his arm around her waist. He looked into Lydia's face as the day lightened. *I'm not as brave as I let you think.*

Oh Lord, strengthen us as a family. Keep me strong. Bless Lydia. Help Addie feel more secure and loved. We're in your hands. Jesus' name, Amen.

He lay with his ladies on either side of him. Their honeymoon cocoon was about to open on a full-fledged butterfly.

⁂

The next morning they rode in silence, each lost in thought, and hopeful of reaching Franklin. Addie was lulled to sleep in Douglas' arms.

"Just around the bend now." They plodded along the washed roadway, picking their way over fallen trees, trash, scoured sand and rock.

"Douglas, I don't see the town! *Where's Franklin?*"

She looked around, "*It's gone!* This is where it's supposed to be, but look at those big trees and all the debris. This place has been flooded out."

"If Boonville wasn't directly south across the river from us, I'd think we were in the wrong place," Douglas pointed at

Boonville. "Look up there on the hillside, there's several houses left on the higher ground and you can see tracks where things have been dragged away. There's some foundation stones here, so this has to be the town's site. There must have been a colossal flood through here not too long ago."

"My folks couldn't write us, because we were on the road. I hope everyone is safe. Do you suppose the townspeople knew it was coming and got away?"

"I don't know why not. Floods usually creep in over a period of days, or hours at least, so they would have ample warning to save themselves and their animals. A flood this large would make a noise with the water flow, they'd be bound to hear it, even if it happened at night," Douglas soothed Lydia's fears.

"Let's ride up the hill and see if we can find someone that knows more than we do about this. My curiosity is getting the better of me."

Addie was awakening in Douglas' arms, she stirred and sleepily looked around at the desolation.

"How you doing, Addie?" Douglas asked. "We aren't paying much attention to you, we're so busy looking at where Franklin used to be. It looks like slicked over mud and sand, with big trees washed in on top. Look at that gravel hill, over there."

"We'll fix you a sand pile and you can play in it when we get home. That'll be so much fun," Lydia attempted to distract Addie and allay her own feelings of fear.

"We better get on to your folks, they'll be glad to see you."

"They'll be glad to see us all. Oh, Douglas, I'll be glad to see them. All of a sudden, I'm so homesick I can hardly stand it. Maybe it's because I'm worried about them. Let's go."

"There's no livery stable here in Franklin to leave the mule. He's still carrying our baggage, guess he has to come along with us this time."

"Let's go faster. Addie likes to ride fast. She doesn't mind galloping. Let's go." Lydia turned Ribbon's head toward high ground, and squeezed with her heel. The animal's feet sucked in the mud of desolation. They rode uphill to the prairie on the north.

Douglas followed behind Lydia, with the little girl.

The mule trailed behind Lydia's horse. He'd formed an attachment for the mare and stayed close, even when off his lead rope. It was well that the packs were firmly anchored, he gave a series of bucks as he ran along behind.

This was the fastest they'd gone while on the trail and the animals got into the spirit of play along with their owners, *running from destruction, to family.*

Lydia's mare recognized the scent of home and needed no guiding.

Surprise!

"Addie, we're on our way to my mother and father's. You'll like it there. We'll have such fun with my brothers. You know, I told you their names and all about them?"

"Mommy, will they be white?"

Lydia blanched and didn't know what to say. *I didn't expect this. How am I to explain to her?* Douglas came to her rescue.

"Yes, they're white, but that doesn't matter, they're your family and mine too. I married your mommy and I'm your daddy and they are your Grandpa and Grandma Williams. Mommy's brothers are your uncles. Won't that be nice to have a big family like that?"

Addie didn't look sure and turned her face to Douglas' shoulder. She clutched her corncob dolly tighter than ever.

Lydia slowed her horse and turned her face to look at Douglas. She had a worried look and mouthed over the little girl's head. "I hope what you said is all true."

"It will be, don't worry. Let's slow down our horses and pray as we ride the last quarter mile."

"I'm glad you thought of that. It's a wonderful idea and we'll have these last couple of minutes together, just our little family."

"Honey, there's where Lydia grew up. It's such a wonderful place. Look there's the guineas and the chickens in the yard there. Guineas say pu-u-ut-reck, pu-u-ut-reck, they sound so funny. There's where I played ball with your mommy and her brothers the first time I came for Sunday dinner with them. Let's turn in here at the barn. We can unsaddle the horses and make them happy, then we'll go up and see Mommy's family."

Lydia dismounted and reached for Addie. She cradled the

little girl protectively in her arms, knowing that she would be frightened with new people for awhile and wondered what her family would think of the new addition.

Douglas led the animals to empty stalls and hung the saddles and bridles on the harness trees along the opposite wall. He set the packs on the ground and led the mule into the last stall. Hay was in the mangers, and the animals had recently been watered at Franklin. He closed the last stall door and dropped the latches.

"Lydia and Douglas, I thought that was — My, what have we here?" Mrs. Williams covered her confusion, as she reached for the little girl in Lydia's arms.

"She's shy, maybe you'd better wait a moment. This is Ruth Curry, but she's called Addie. She was an orphan in St. Charles and we couldn't pass her by. I hope you'll all understand our feelings for her when you get to know her better. Addie, this is my mother. Here, you go to Douglas, I need to hug my mommy." Lydia handed Addie to Douglas.

Lydia reached for her mother, "I missed you so much. What happened to Franklin? I was so worried about you all when I saw that awful place."

"We had unusually high water and the channel changed, it took several days, but the water ate away at the town, until almost everything was gone. The few remaining build-ings and usable things have been moved to higher ground and they've left what little ground is left with all that mess. No one wants to bother with it."

"Was everyone saved when Franklin flooded?"

"Yes, there was ample warning. Some carried off their belongings and what they could, but the water started to wash off the bank and the whole river moved over into the town before the flood was over and went back down."

Addie started to squirm.

Mrs. Williams gripped her apron. "Here, where are my manners? You, all must be tired, let's go to the house and I'll get you something to eat and drink. You can rest and tell me all about your trip. Papa and the boys are in the fields, but they'll be in for dinner. Come to think of it, I'd better get in and get it ready or they'll have to go hungry. Come on inside."

"Douglas, you go on, I'll take Addie by the outhouse and we'll be right in."

Lydia's mother and Douglas walked toward the house, their easy relationship resumed from the day of the wedding. Lydia breathed a sigh of relief and sat Addie on the ground.

"Let's go to the outhouse, then we can go in and help my mother get dinner for my brothers and Papa. Would you like that? Maybe you can help me do whatever Mother needs us to. We could set the table, after we wash up. Do you know how to set a table?"

"Yes, Mommy, I used to help my mom— before she went away, I'd help her set the table."

"You asked me if my family would be white? Was your family white or brown?"

"My other mommy was white."

"What about your papa?"

"I didn't know my papa. My other mommy said he died before I was bornd-ed."

"Oh, I'm sorry, but I sure am glad that Douglas and I are your mommy and papa now. I love you, and God willing, we'll never leave you without a family again." Lydia hugged the little girl as she lifted her off the bench. They closed the door, held hands and walked together into Lydia's girlhood home.

"Here we are Mother. We'll wash up, then can we help?"

"She's already got me peeling potatoes, so you'll have to do something else this time," Douglas said. He winked at Addie when he put a drop of water on her nose.

"You girls can set the table and get some chairs from the dining room. When the men are working, we eat in the kitchen, as you remember."

"I like it in the kitchen. It's my favorite room in this whole house. We used to sit here and sew, or anything else that needed to be done. Mommy and I would talk as we worked. Sometimes, I'd go out and help my papa do his work. I'd milk the cow or help him harness the horses. I liked to curry Ribbon and the work horses, but I couldn't always reach as high as they stood."

"Curry?"

"Yes, Curry is your last name, but this kind of curry means to comb out the horse's hair. Papa would have to finish their backs for me, or throw me up on them and I'd work from there. I still couldn't reach their ears or their faces, unless I scooted up their necks. Sometimes, they'd put their faces down so I could reach their forelocks. That's the hair at the top of their faces. When they had burrs from the fields, they wouldn't bend down. You know burrs are stickery and it hurt the horses when I pulled them out of their tails or mane. They didn't like to have the burrs, but they didn't like me pulling their hair either. Does that sound like someone else you know?"

"Not Papa, but Addie don't like hair pull."

"You're right. You and Ribbon don't like to have your hair pulled when I comb out the tangles."

"Here, baby, can you put this on the table for me?"

Lydia looked at her mother's response with a smile over Addie's head.

"I'm no baby."

"How old are you?"

"Umh, Mommy says I'm four."

"I think she's about right. You look four to me and I've raised four children that passed by the four-year mark. Lydia, do you know when her birthday is? We'll have to bake her a cake."

"No, we don't. Let's just choose a date and celebrate. How about that?"

"Well, how about tomorrow? That will give us time to get a fancy cake baked and get everything ready for a party. Would you like to have Saturday, August 10 for your birthday?"

"What's a birfday?"

"It's the day you were born, then each year you have another one. We figure you're ready for your fourth one, so tomorrow you would be four and then August 10, a year from now, you'll be five and on, until you get as old as me. Would that be okay?"

"I think so, but I don't want to get old and die, like my mommy did."

Lydia's mother knelt to look into Addie's eyes.

"Oh, you poor child. You're going to live a long time and

so are Douglas and Lydia. We're all going to take care of you and so will God."

The little girl reached out and put her hand on Mrs. Williams' cheek.

"Don't be sad. You can have my dolly, then you'll feel all better."

Mrs. Williams slowly placed her hand on the child's shoulder and drew her into an embrace. Addie's little arms went round her neck and she laid her head on her new grandmother's shoulder.

"Thank you, Mother." Lydia wrapped her arms around her mother and the sweet child. Douglas wiped his wet hands and hugged the three.

"Papa, don't cry."

"Honey, we're happy, we're not sad. Sometimes when people are *really* happy, they cry, but these are happy tears," Douglas patted her on the back.

"I'm not cryin' and I'm happy," Addie said.

"I know, different people show that they are happy in different ways, but that's all right. You show how you feel the way you want to and we'll show we're happy the way we want to." Lydia smiled and the other three did too.

Mrs. Williams wiped her cheek with her apron. "We'd better finish up this meal, or we'll have some hungry men in here before long."

"They won't mind, they'll be happy too, so maybe we'll spend the afternoon being happy together. I hope they can take some time off to be with us all. I want her to get acquainted with the men in this family," Lydia said.

"She will Honey," Douglas soothed. "We've got all the time in the world for that. She's going to be overwhelmed when they all come in at once. It will really be better if she meets them separately or a few at a time."

"Well, they'll all come at once, so we don't have that choice."

"I could carry her out to the field and then she could look at them as they come in. That way she could see them at a distance, before we all get together at once."

"Yes, Douglas, I think that's a good idea." She turned to the child, "Do you want to have Papa carry you to the field? You can see the big horses working and you can tell the men that it's almost time for dinner. You can call them in like a big girl."

"Yes, Papa, go."

Douglas hoisted the little girl onto his shoulders, tried to put his hat on her head and they went out the door, ducking to miss the jamb. Addie giggled.

"Lydia, that's the sweetest child. What ever possessed any family to give her up?"

"We don't know much about her, other than she's an orphan and there is no one left in her family. We got her in St. Charles. Two unrelated men had her and they didn't want her, so we got a bill of sale and took her. I couldn't stand to see her so dirty and they didn't care a thing for her. She was like a frightened bunny rabbit when we got her. I'm afraid she's been mistreated sometime, but we don't know. She's afraid of strangers and she didn't talk very well. At first we thought she was trying to say *Daddy*, but the men told us they called her Addie, so that's what we call her. She said her papa was dead before she was born. The bill of sale papers we got, say that her name is Ruth Curry and her parents are deceased. As far as we're concerned she's our adopted daughter and we intend to raise her as our own child. That seems to suit her, so as you say, *That's that*." Lydia was out of breath.

"Bill of Sale?"

"Yes, Mother. We bought her. She was being sold as a slave, but Addie says her mother was white. She never saw her father. We washed her and she's much whiter than we thought at first. She said the men rubbed black stuff on her and we're not sure she is a Negro. It doesn't matter to Douglas and me."

"Poor child."

"That's the way I felt, and I couldn't bear to leave her with no one who cared about her."

"You can tell she's a sympathetic little thing and I'd say that she's smart, but she hasn't had the best, that's obvious too."

"We're trying to make that up to her and she's come a long way already. I think she'll forget the bad things that have happened to her and be fine, before long. We intend to try anyway. We're going to change her last name to Charlton, so that won't hang over her all the time as a reminder and we're not mentioning how we got her." Lydia put her hand on her mother's arm, "Mother, we do love her."

"I can see that and I can also see why."

"Thanks for accepting her and being kind to her."

"Daughter, you thought I wouldn't be kind to her? How could you think a thing like that about me with any child?"

"I'm sorry Mother, but I know she's a shock and we didn't know how you'd react to your own daughter and her husband having a four year-old child with a strange background. You didn't even know about Addie until we sprung her on you. I guess I'm a little defensive about her."

"I would say that's the way a woman should be about her children. You're a grown woman. I think this is a good decision and I pray everything goes as you hope it will. I'll certainly help in every way I can." She hugged her daughter, "I'm so glad you're home and made the long trip safely. You'll have to tell me all about it when we get these men and their dinner out of the way."

"Thank you, Mother. I'm very glad to be home, Douglas and I *are very happy*. Kentucky wasn't the way I expected, but I'm at peace over *most* of it. I'll tell you more about it a little later. Douglas isn't from the kind of family I expected."

Her mother drew in a quick breath.

"Oh, don't look startled, I don't mean in a bad way. They're very wealthy, they own two plantations and many slaves. The slaves are the idea that I have the most trouble with. That's one reason we don't intend to tell anyone, other than this family, that we bought Addie."

"Douglas doesn't flaunt any wealth, he lives very conservatively."

"I know Mother. That is one reason I was so surprised when I saw Fairbank the first time. It's huge. Douglas has a trust, from his Grandmother Sidwell, but he's not interested in the plantation's money. We will use some of his funds to build a home for ourselves, then we intend to live on his teaching salary."

"He feels called to teach and never intends to go back to his planter life for a living. We'll visit, but our life is here, or wherever Douglas chooses to teach at the moment. We don't want the money."

Lydia continued, "Frankly, I didn't understand plantation life or the institution of slavery. I thought I knew about slavery, but Missouri slavery is not like plantation slavery. Maybe in some places in Missouri, like up around Lexington or in the Mississippi River country it is more like Kentucky plantation life, but not here. Not unless I've had my eyes closed. I'm certainly going to look around here. I'm not going to take things dealing with slavery for granted again," Lydia took a deep breath.

"I guess we're all a little blind to things that we're not directly involved with. We tend to overlook the familiar, you know, seeing the splinter in another's eye, while we've got a log in our own?" Lydia's mother commented.

"I think you're right."

"Here, the potatoes are ready, I'll get them mashed and you can make the gravy. I see the men coming this way. Look, Addie's riding on your father's work mare. She looks kind of small up there, but look at her bouncing up and down."

"That's one thing she's not afraid of. She likes our horses and she thinks she can ride alone, but we don't let her. I think she'll make a wonderful horsewoman someday. She's got a good start. Oops, I'd better stir this gravy, or it will be lumpy."

"It looks like your father made a hit with her by letting her ride Brownie in."

"I expect Douglas encouraged him in that. He knows what it takes to get her mind off her fear of strangers. He could put that bug into Papa's ear real quick."

"He's very thoughtful, isn't he?"

"Yes, Mommy, he's the grandest man, excluding my own papa, I've ever known."

"That's as it should be. A wife should feel her husband is the most wonderful man on earth."

Fall
An Old Acquaintance

"Lydia, your father said that Mr. Becknell opened a livery stable over in Boonville when Franklin was washed away. I can take the mule over there to return him."

"Good idea, the mule's not working now and perhaps Mr. Becknell needs him."

"I'll ride over and see when the Academies open and get a few arrangements made."

"Hurry back. It's great here with the family, but I think it's about time we got our own home set up."

"I wasn't sure if you still felt that way?"

"Yes, we need to live in Boonville, so why don't you look for houses while you're over there? If you find anything, we can go over later and see it. I love you. Hurry back."

Douglas kissed her and dropped a peck on the top of Addie's head.

"I'll be back in a little while. Help your mommy and grandma while I'm gone."

When he arrived home, Douglas hurried onto the porch, where Addie and Lydia sat in the swing.

"I saw a poster at Mr. Becknell's livery stable. It said, "Half Cent Reward for the return of my apprentice, Christopher "Kit" Houston Carson.""

"You mean that young man who came and listened to the stories of the Santa Fe Trail?" Lydia asked.

"Yes, I guess the harness maker finally gave up on him and decided the boy was going to make good on his interest in going west."

"He must not have wanted him back very badly to only offering half a cent for his return.:

"I think it was inevitable that Kit would go west, his boss was just waiting for it to happen. Douglas added,"He doesn't have much to hold him here any longer. He's one of the younger members of his family and most of them have moved on in their lives."

I hope the boy can be happy and will have a good life," Lydia said.

"You'll never guess who else I saw in Boonville?" Douglas said.

"One of the graduates of the Academies?"

"No. Johnny, one of the first fellows I taught to read when I came to Franklin. I ran into him at the general store and he said they just got in from Santa Fe the day before yesterday. He looked tired, but he surely was glad to see me."

"How did things go for him?"

"Johnny said they made extra good money, but there is a rumor that the starting point for the Santa Fe Trail will be moved to Arrow Rock or Westport next year, even though the Boonville one keeps them away from the difficult crossing at Arrow Rock."

"Are they moving it for sure?"

"No, he said it was a rumor, but freight gets to Westport easier now on the river and he thought it would shorten their travel time by moving the beginning further west. It sounds logical, but I guess we'll find out soon enough. When Franklin flooded away, it caused changes. Many of the 1500 or so people have moved and the whole town of Boonville has changed because of it. It's crowded over there. The only place I could find to live was in one room at the old Boone's Lick House and it wasn't much. There wouldn't be any place for Addie to play outside."

"I was thinking things would be like it had always been, but I can see how there would have to be changes with all those people being without homes."

"We can build a new house with part of my trust. I did find some sites not too far from the Academies that we could buy. Do you suppose your folks would let us stay here for a few months, until we can get something arranged? Or would you even want to ask?"

"I do want our own home, but it wouldn't be so bad to

stay here for awhile, if it suits everyone. Let's ask and see what they say."

"I wonder if your father would be interested in hiring on to help with the building, after he gets his crops in this fall? He's got things in good shape here and he could work over there when he wants to. Do you think he'd be offended if we asked?"

"He's very open, we can ask and he can decide. You won't be offended, if he doesn't want to, will you?"

"No, I just thought that might hurry things along a little."

"How long would it take to build a house?"

"That would depend on how big and fancy we want it."

"I can see we've got many things to consider, and here I thought you went into town on a simple matter."

"I found out other things by listening too. There isn't much enthusiasm for rebuilding Franklin. The flood frightened people and they saw the problem of building that close to the river again when the land is so low. Boonville stands on higher ground and there's more rock. Franklin was on a flood plain and was mostly silt soil. When the flood waters rose, it sloughed the ground away and even took some loamy hills along. There wasn't any foundation under that deep soil. If they move the starting point of the Santa Fe Trail, there won't be much purpose for having a new town so close to the water and Boonville."

"My, it's so different in just a few months. I never dreamed we'd come home to so many changes," Lydia commented.

"You're right— married, getting Addie, no town of Franklin, and finding a place to live. Our situation has changed remarkably, but I like most of it. I would never wish for a town to wash away, but the rest is fine, in fact, it's very fine."

"Something else too, Douglas."

"I thought I named everything, what else?"

"We're going to have another child in the late spring. I've been pretty sure, but I didn't want to tell you until I was certain."

"Oh, Lydia, I love you," he hugged her tenderly. "Everything you do makes me so happy. I must be the happiest man I know."

"I'm about the happiest woman and we've got Addie too, it's just more than I can imagine."

"Just about the happiest? Why not *the* happiest?"

"Give me another hug, then you'll be one hundred percent right and of course, I *will be* the happiest woman alive."

New Home

"Lydia, I met with Mr. Byron. He has two artisans that help him make bricks. We talked over plans and he says that they are able to make exactly what I want for our new house. He even came to look over the possible sites. The one nearest the Academies has that outcropping of rock and he thinks they could use that stone for the foundation. He can have the clay hauled in and they can make the bricks on the property. They'd set up a brick kiln on the side closest to the river and could move the clay in from down the river, to the lower side of the property. The bricks could be fired there. That way, they'd get the shape and measurements more accurate."

"Douglas, I didn't know we were that far along with our plans, we haven't talked about the kind of home we want. What kind were you thinking of?"

"I thought we'd build a smaller version of The Valley Plantation House, except we'd put brick columns out front, rather than those white ones they have in Kentucky. We could cap them with white to match the other trim on the verandahs and possibly put on shutters."

"That house is beautiful, but it's kind of big and fancy for us, and Boonville."

"No, there are more and more southern style homes in Boonville and we'll make ours smaller. Maybe four main rooms downstairs and four upstairs, with an attic over the upstairs. We'd put in a central hall, with stairway. Then we could put a kitchen wing on the back. Just imagine how beautiful it would be coming up from the river."

"That sounds good. I was afraid you'd want it too big."

"No, it doesn't have to be as big as The Valley. On my

salary, we can't afford anything like that, but I'd like plenty of room for the family we'll have someday."

"Won't it be fun, sitting on the verandah in the summer, watching the river with boats coming and going?"

"I think the columns made from brick will be of special interest. You know that most builders can't build cylindrical columns. This builder has figured out how to mold the bricks in half-moons with the corners off, so the bricks fit just right. Otherwise, they'd have to cut the inside corner of the bricks or have big grooves between the bricks with extra mortar."

"Who did you say the builder was?"

"Mr. Byron."

"Oh, Douglas, he uses slaves when he builds."

"Of course, didn't you know that?"

"Yes, I've seen some of his buildings upriver and in Boon-ville, but— can't we build without slaves?"

"Lydia, I've talked to Mr. Byron and he has agreed to build the house for the amount of money that I think we can afford. If we use a builder without slaves, it will cost us more than we can manage. And he gives his artisans a half cent for every brick they make and lay. Most slave owners don't pay their slaves anything."

"How much would they make on our house?"

"By the time they build the house and lay the fence, the two men should make around one hundred and fifty dollars each."

"How long will it take for them to buy their freedom?"

"I don't think Mr. Byron will release them while he's able to build, but when he gets older, he might. They can buy their families and save up for their later life."

"Is that the best he can do for them?"

"I think so. This process that he's come up with to build the curved bricks is very important. They know his process and are invaluable to him. He's had them for years and they work along beside him. He doesn't ask them to do anything that he's not willing to do himself. I talked with others that he's built for. I knew you wouldn't like us using slave labor to build our new home. The three work more like equals, I don't think you'll mind this arrangement."

"I hope you're right Douglas. You know I'm not happy about slaves working on our new home, but I guess that's what we'll have to do."

"Thank you, Lydia. I'll stop by each day and see that everyone is treated the way we would want them to be. You can come often too, if you want. We can go down in the evenings and look things over."

"You don't want me here in the daytime?"

"Lydia, I don't mind if you stop by, but you have to remember that we're having a baby and you're going to be very busy before long. You may not want to ride Ribbon, or even in the buggy before too long."

"Oh, you're right. I guess I will increase in breadth before long, won't I?" The humor lightened the seriousness of their home planning.

"That's what usually happens with expectant mothers." Douglas gave Lydia a hug, "That way, there will be more of you for me to love."

"You're planning a fence too?" She was distracted, and ignored his reference to her waistline.

"Yes, we'd be too close to the river. I don't want to constantly worry about the children falling in. They should be able to play outside and have the opportunity to do things on their own as they get older. The best site I found, slopes down toward the Missouri, then falls off that limestone bluff. You remember how it felt in that current. We can't take a chance with our family."

◆

A month later, Mr. Byron and his two slave artisans floated their equipment down the river and landed on the site of Douglas and Lydia's new home. They moved in bricks to build a tunnel kiln on the property and stockpiled sand from Franklin, to mix in their mortar.

"All those tools don't make the river view wonderful, but that part won't last forever. They'll tear down the kiln and move everything when they finish," Douglas commented when he brought Lydia to see the beginnings.

"I close my eyes, when I imagine looking up the hill, I can

see our new home. Look at those wonderful trees in the back part of the lawn. They will make a good place for the children to play. We can put a sand pile there, swings in the trees and there is even room for a little barn for our animals. We can have a cow for fresh milk, our horses and pets. Douglas, I can hardly wait!"

"It will take about a year to finish the house, you've got your job cut out for you now. We'll get this baby born and started before we move in. That will be good, because your mother can help you now. You'll be strong by the time we are on our own again."

"Yes, it is wonderful to be with my family and have Mother there when I have questions. She doesn't interfere with us and Addie, but she's there when I need her. It's been good to be with them since we've been back."

"I wish you and my mother could be that close, but I know there is nothing like your *own* mother. I understand how you feel about her. She's a wonderful woman, even if she is my mother in law."

"Douglas, I'm glad that you're not jealous of my family's relationship with me. I know that some men don't like living with their wife's family and being under their eyes all the time. Thank you for being so understanding."

"They make it easier for me. If I need to stay at school in the evening, I won't worry about you and Addie. I know you're safe and not lonely. We've got plenty of time to be alone after the house is built. When it's ready, you'll be so close, I could look out the window of the Academies and see you on the lawn. We could even work out a signal, so we could communicate during the day."

"Yes, I could hang a towel out the bedroom window and you could tell it was time for supper, like we do at home when Mother wants to call the men in from the field."

"We could even change the colors, to give different messages. Let's see? Pink would mean, *I love you*, blue could mean, *I miss you*, yellow- "

"Here, if you don't watch out, you're going to embarrass me! You know how big people's eyes and ears are. They'd soon wonder what was going on. Remember, you *do have a job*."

"But they'd be our *secret* colors, no one else would know what they meant."

Across the Wide Missouri

Mr. Byron and his men slapped the wet clay mixture into the molds and troweled off the excess to smooth the back. They moved down the line to turn over another row of dried bricks and stacked those on racks to pull into the kiln. Those who witnessed the activity, were fascinated by the process of making the final bricks to finish the round columns on the veranda.

It pained Lydia to watch the two artisan slaves, as they worked on forming the bricks from the red clay. She listened to the banter of Mr. Byron and the two. They sounded happy, but she also saw a sadness in the eyes of the two colored men even though they seldom looked her in the face.

After the birth of her son in the early summer, she drove to the building site each afternoon and waited there for Douglas' arrival. Addie sometimes went along, but the baby stayed with his grandmother. It was Baby John and Grandma's special time together when he awakened just before Lydia's family arrived back at her parent's home each day.

Addie had lost her fear of the two slaves that worked for Mr. Byron. Lydia wondered if it was their friendliness to Addie or if frequent association caused her to forget. Addie couldn't say, probably didn't know. Lydia was grateful for the healing that time had given the growing girl.

Lydia and Addie washed the windows, swept out the sawdust and impatiently awaited the final days of building. She stayed out of the way of the workmen, but carried fresh lemonade or refreshments each trip to the house. This was her only contact each day with the workmen, when she offered the men a cooling break for their labors through August and September.

*I feel the need to thank these men. Slaves, what a
terrible word. I am so grateful to them and am sorry for their
condition. I can't do much for them, but I want them to know
how I feel. My opportunities are almost gone.*

Mr. Byron left for downtown Boonville as Lydia arrived
during the last Wednesday, of the final week of construction. He
waved as Lydia drove onto the graveled driveway in the rear. She
tied Ribbon to the hitching rail, alighted with Addie, and lifted out
the basket of refreshments. The two walked to where one of the
two artisans held a board while the other planed. The curly shav-
ings rolled smoothly from the sharp blade of the plane.

"Are you men thirsty?"

The older of the two looked at her and nodded. He looked
down at Addie. The little girl fidgeted near the curls from the
smooth board.

"Little Missy want a curl?

"Can I, Mommy?"

"Sure, get as many as you want. We'll probably burn
them anyway."

Addie heaped the curls into her apron skirt and went to sit
on the porch steps. She laid out the curls in a row and examined
each minutely. Lydia watched her, then turned to the men. She
poured out the glasses of cool lemonade.

"I want to tell you that I was against having slaves build
this house."

The men looked shocked, then embarrassed.

She continued, "I'm against slavery, but like you, I don't
have much control. I'm grateful for the wonderful work you did
on our home. I may not have another opportunity to thank you for
being such fine workmen. I hope this work helps you buy your
own and your families' freedom. Here is a small gift from Addie
and me.." She handed the men each an envelope with a gold
Spanish coin inside.

"Remember that I am thinking about you and your
families and I'll be praying for you, *all*, as you move from this job
when you finish the fence. God Bless you both." She turned to

leave. She wasn't sure how the two would take her statements and gift. She didn't wish to put them on the spot.

"Miss Lydia, we thanks you. You been kind to us while we been here. We'll remember you too. We be prayin' for you family."

The younger man added, "Thank you, God Bless you, you fine husband and you babies."

Lydia smiled and turned to go.

Addie looked up at the men, she smiled shyly and spoke, "Thank you for my curls."

"You welcome, Missy. Take good care of yo' brother when you move in here."

ठ♣

It was beautiful October. The house was finished. It faced eastward looking out over the hills toward bright fall costumed bluffs, flamed by the sunset. The night before the move, the little family of four, stood on the upstairs front balcony and looked down upon the Missouri River to the north, as it carried its load of water and silt toward the east.

"It couldn't be more beautiful, Douglas."

"What, the house or the river hills?"

"Both. God has decorated our domain more beautifully than we could ever do on our own. He's painted it all new and perfect for us. When I come up from the river, the trees behind the house, formed a burnished frame. They fit together so nicely. The green of the trees in summer fits too."

"Lydia and Addie, let's kneel here with baby John, and dedicate our new home to God's glory."

The adults knelt, with Addie tucked on Douglas' knee. Lydia held baby John against her shoulder as Douglas prayed.

"Dear God, we dedicate this house to your glory. Help everyone who enters or dwells within to live for you. Help us as we go about our daily tasks to do your will. Bless this family. Allow, and help us to be a light in this community, to live in the way that you would have us live and to be a blessing to others. Help us to use this house for you. Lord, help our children to give their lives to you, when they are old enough to understand. Keep us safe and well, if it be your will. Direct our lives. Thank you

Father, for these blessings that you've given to our family and each member here. Bless any that may come in the future and keep us ever close to you. In Jesus' name, Amen."

"Papa, look, the sun's hitting our family. We're in His light!"

"Yes, do you think that is God's sign to us, that He is with our family?"

"Yes, Papa, just like Samson and Ben said."

"How did you know their names?"

"I asked them."

Douglas looked at Lydia and smiled. The family stood together on the balcony until the shadow of the house covered the lawn and the beautiful light faded. They waited until the stars appeared.

Douglas turned his family. He took Addie's hand in his; gripped Lydia's elbow and they descended the stairs and out the back of their new home.

Tomorrow was moving day and they needed an early start.

Eighteen Months Later
Annoyance

A dark head peered over the wall, while Douglas trimmed the grass around the big trees on the lawn.

"Hello, Kirk, how are you?"

The head jerked down and disappeared. Douglas reached the fence and looked over at a retreating back.

"I didn't mean to scare you. Come on back and we can talk." No response, he shook his head and went back to his yard work.

I didn't mean to frighten him off. That boy's as skittish as a spring colt, I'll have to ask Lydia if she's seen him around. Douglas soon forgot the incident in the completion of his job.

Addie followed baby John as he toddled down the hill. The two-year old gurgled as he raced ahead of Addie to reach his father first. Out of reach, he looked back and tumbled at his father's feet, squealing with delight.

"Here, fellow, watch where you're going," Douglas tossed the baby into the air, pretending to throw him. "You won, you're going to be a fast one."

Addie stood back, looking at her two favorite men.

Douglas shifted John to his left arm and reached out for Addie, willing her into the circle of his embrace.

"My two favorite children. What's on your minds this afternoon?"

Addie snuggled against him comfortably, "Momma says that supper is ready and we came to get you."

"Great, shall we run up the hill and see who wins this time?"

Addie took off without waiting for them. She knew her papa was a good runner. Reaching the verandah steps ahead of the two, she whirled around the hitching post to see how far they were behind her. Papa had slowed down to toss John up again. The pair whooped with laughter.

Douglas gave her curl a fond pull, "You won that time, but just wait until this young man grows up a little, then he'll give you a run for your money."

Content, Douglas looked back down over the lawn and caught a glimpse of that same dark head disappearing below the wall again.

"Addie, do you ever see Kirkland Simms when you're out playing?"

"He looks over the wall."

"Very often?"

"Every day or so."

"Does he ever say anything?"

"No."

"Nothing at all?"

"Sometimes he makes faces, if we look at him."

"Hum, what do you make of that?"

"He doesn't hurt us. I think he's cur— wants to see what we're doing."

"You're probably right. His father keeps him busy at the store, so don't guess he's around too much." Douglas made a mental note to ask Lydia if the boy caused any trouble.

After putting the children to bed, Lydia and Douglas lay cradled in each others arms in their big canopied bed enjoying quiet talk.

"Douglas, does it ever worry you that Addie is so quiet around other people?"

"Yes, her big blue eyes take in everything, but she keeps it to herself. I'd like to know what is going on inside her head— but I think she's happy."

"She does talk to me when she's worried, but being talkative around others is not her nature. Do you suppose it goes back to when she was a baby?" Lydia turned to look at her husband's face in the moonlight.

"I don't know. In some ways, she isn't any more quiet than some of my students, but it's hard for me to tell. Because I love her, I can't be objective."

"Do you think we ought to ask someone else if she's too quiet?"

"I'll visit with her teacher and see what he thinks. He sees her with other children, maybe she talks more to them than we think."

"He says she knows the answers when he asks her a question, but I already knew she was smart."

"I doubt that she volunteers answers on her own."

"You're probably right. When will you visit with him?"

"Maybe tomorrow after my classes dismiss. I'll walk by his room before I come home."

"I hope he doesn't feel we're checking on him or have any complaints."

"I know him very well, I don't think he'll feel that. That reminds me, do you see Kirk Simms peeping over the wall when you're outside?"

"You mean Adrian Simms' oldest boy? He looks over at the children every few days. He seems lonely to me. Maybe he'd like to come in and play with Addie and John."

"I saw him twice today. The last time was after I caught him looking and he ran off."

"Really? That's strange."

"Invite him in, if you want to, but I'd keep an eye out— don't want him teasing the little ones. Addie said he sometimes makes faces at them."

The family was not able to catch Kirk Simms, he scampered out of sight each time they saw him.

Douglas stopped by Simms Mercantile and spoke to Kirk as he swept the front boardwalk.

"Kirk, if you would like to come inside our lawn and play sometime, that would be fine with Mrs. Charlton and me."

The boy flashed a startled look at Douglas' face, then glanced quickly over to seek his father's whereabouts. Douglas looked to see Mr. Simms go into the back room, then looked back at Kirk. The boy had moved away and swept more vigorously. *Impolite or scared? Hard to say. I'll have to try again, another time.* "So long, Kirk."

The boy looked down at his broom and didn't seem to hear.

ಶಿ

While little John took his afternoon nap, Lydia stepped to the back door and spoke to Addie, "Run up to Mr. Simms' store and get me a bag of flour. I need to finish this bread before Papa gets home. Here's the money. I'll stand right here where I can see you go into the store and I can hear John if he wakes up. If I'm not here when you come out of the store, come right home. I'll be in the kitchen or getting John. It's about time for him to wake up."

Addie looked at her mother and at the store. "I see Miss Mary. I'll hurry right back, Momma."

Lydia watched as Addie darted up the street. "That child runs like a scared deer, graceful and free on her feet. This errand won't take her long at that speed."

John let out a loud screech.

"Oh, dear, I'll have to go get that young man." Lydia glanced up the street and hurried inside the back door.

Addie stopped just outside the mercantile door and looked inside. No one was in sight. She tiptoed inside the open door and walked toward the counter, ready to call for Mrs. Simms. There was a banging in the back room. Addie began to back cautiously toward the entry.

"Boy, when I tell you to do something, you do it. You hear me?"

Addie heard the unmistakable whack of a stick and a quick gasp escaped her lips. The sound came again and again. Muffled sobs sounded from the back room. It sounded like a struggle. She heard a whimpering voice, knew that it belonged to Kirk. Turning, she started for the boardwalk.

Mr. Simms' voice yelled from the back room.

"Get your self out there and do that job and don't let me have to tell you again."

Feet scrambled behind her and Kirk sped past. He turned

outside the door and looked back. He gave her a look of such hatred, that she shrank back against the store window. He disappeared from sight. Addie looked tentatively toward home.

Momma wanted flour, but I'm afraid to go back in there.

She looked down the street and saw her mother standing on the back porch holding John's hand. Footsteps sounded behind her. She turned and saw Miss Mary walk to the front of the store. Addie followed her and hurried to the counter.

"What do you want?" Mr. Simms was blunt.

"My momma wants a bag of bread flour."

"Well, speak up!" Mr. Simms turned for the bag of flour and plopped it on the counter. Flour dust exploded from the outside of the cloth bag.

Addie laid the money on the counter. He handed her back a few pennies. She picked up the flour and pennies, then turned and exited as quickly as she could without running.

I'm glad Mama is watching for me. He's scary.

Lydia watched Addie as she carefully carried the bag of flour in her arms. "You look worried, are you all right?"

"Here's the flour."

"Yes, I see that. You did a good job. I can take it from here. I expect that feels kind of heavy?"
"No, it was fine."

Lydia tilted Addie's face up and looked into her eyes. "You're a good girl, Addie. Thanks for your help. John woke up and he would have cried if one of us wasn't here to get him. You're my big girl now and Momma needs you."

Addie hugged her mother's legs and hid her eyes. Lydia reached to turn her toward the back door, then patted her shoulder, preoccupied with her delayed bread making.

After Douglas came from the Academies, she said, "Addie went to the store for me today. I stood outside the back door and watched her to the store while I waited for John to wake up. She got this bread flour for me all by herself."

"That's our big helper, we're proud of you, Addie."

Addie blushed and looked away. Douglas reached out to pat her shoulder and then over her head for another slice of the yeasty, hot bread.

≥▲

After the humiliation of his back room threshing, Kirk's hatred for Addie grew. He was sure that she had overheard by the horrified look on her face as he raced past her. He had no control over his father, but he could handle a little mouse like Addie.

She's always lookin' at me with those big eyes. I know what's going on in her head. She's laughin' at me. One of these days, I'll show her who's better. I hate my father, even more than I hate her. He's always nice-e-nice to his customers and then beats on me. Someday, I'll get him too. "Respected member of the community," that's what the paper said when they ran that piece about the store. They don't know much. He ain't half as respected as they think.

As time passed, anger fanned higher and hotter in the tortured boy's heart. He was more determined and more stealthy in his spying on the Charlton family. Schemes ran through his head, as he planned his revenge.

She thinks she's too good to talk to me. She don't talk to nobody, but those girls at school and her brother. I know she sees me sometimes when I peep over her wall. She just looks the other way and goes back toward her house. Rich and snotty, that's her.

She fools everybody with her swee-eet voice and the way she tucks her head, but she thinks she's better'n me. Someday, I'm gonna show her.

At church, he taunted her on her way back from the outhouse.

"Stuck up, think you're so good. You're just a mouse and I'm gonna sic a cat on you!"

Addie ran to the church door where the congregation was taking their leave. In the hustle no one noticed her pale face. Gradually the crowd drifted off to their homes and the incident was not discovered by the adults.

≥▲

Spring rains came and Kirk was tied to the store by the jobs that his father laid out for him. His agitation at his confinement escalated.

The next day at school, when recess came, Kirk hid under their teacher's cloak. When Addie reached for her coat, next to the corner, he leaped out.

"Mouse! Mouse! Growl!"

Addie turned with a startled look and stepped into the corner.

Kirk advanced with a grimace on his face.

"Grr." His fingers curled into claws, "I'll get you!"

Addie ducked into the wall and under his arm. She ran from the cloak room and out the classroom door. The pupils from Miss Wilson's class filed down the hall. Addie walked demurely at the end of their line and to the outside door into the play yard.

Martha ran up "What took you so long? Let's play jacks."

Addie didn't answer, but walked behind Martha to a cleared spot under a tree. She turned to look back toward the school door and saw Kirk come outside. He ran to play ball with some boys from her class.

"Addie, it's your turn. Pay attention!"

All Fall Down

When Kirk could no longer endure his father's over-bearing behavior and the confinement of the rainy day, he whispered to his mother, "Don't we need a mess of fish for supper?"

She raised her voice, good for an excuse, "Kirk, I need some fish for supper. Why don't you go down to the river and see what you can catch?"

His father couldn't deny the family a free supper. He acquiesced to his wife's request without comment, but pursed his mouth into a sour expression.

Kirk knew that his father preferred that he go upriver to fish, but he never failed to go down river, where he walked along the bank of the Missouri, on the outside of Addie's wall. Each time he went by, he couldn't deny himself the pleasure of observing her or the family, but greatly disappointed each time he failed to see her in her white dress, with a blue ribbon sash and her bouncy, golden curls. A pang came into his heart as he looked at the pristine lawn. He could imagine the family playing there, he'd seen them often enough. They're *happy. My family is never joyous or happy.*

Today, the rains made the path slippery; he tried to avoid getting his shoes wet. He surveyed before, and behind him to see if anyone was watching, then stepped off the path. The bank gave way beneath his feet and he slipped toward the river. Kirk dug the end of his pole into the dirt. When the bank crumbled beneath his hands, he dug with his knees and feet; grasped for hanging brush with his hands as he fell, and kept sliding. His body moved over the edge. A sharp pain in his leg made him cry out. He snatched the sturdy trunk of a sprout.

He caught his breath, tried to ease himself back up on top of the bank. It crumbled beneath his one good leg and with each jerk, sent excruciating pain through his injured leg. Sparks flashed before his eyes. *I can't black out, I'd drown for sure.*

Suspended, he hung for fifteen minutes, then longer— the rain came down. The cold rain seeped through his jacket.

I can't hold on much longer, my hands are getting numb and slick. What if these roots give way? I can't move because every time I do, more mud falls. My leg hurts! This sprout is going to pull out of the ground.

He looked below again at the roiling muddy waters.

The river's near flood stage and movin' fast. I'd have a terrible time gettin' out of the water, if I don't hurt myself when I fall. Maybe if I holler again, someone'll hear me.

"Help!" *That wasn't loud enough for anyone to hear.* He took a deep breath. "Help me!"

Addie sat in the porch swing reading. She lifted her head and listened, then resumed her study of the book in her lap.

"Help! Somebody help me!" came faintly.

She stood up, looked toward the wall, walked to the rail, and listened.

"Help!"

The sound was louder now. She walked down the steps and looked over the lawn. "Is someone there?" At first she spoke tentatively.

"Help."

She laid her book on the floor of the veranda and stepped out into the rain.

I'm sure, there's someone calling for help. She ran across the lawn to the wall and looked over. Nothing unusual showed.

"Is someone there?"

Sissy girl, she's not strong enough! "Help, I'm down here."

"Keep talking, I can't see you, but I'll be right there." Addie looked up and down the wall. She saw several rounds of wood that her father had cut from a dead tree; she stacked the rounds and stepped up on the pile. The rounds started to slip, but she had her hands over the top of the wall and heaved herself up, much as she did climbing trees at her grandparent's. She had no trouble scrambling to the top, looked along the bank and saw where it had given way. A cane pole, and what looked like a can of worms, lay at the raw edge.

"I'm coming, hang on." Addie jumped from the wall, her dress caught on the top of the bricks, ripped. When she landed, mud splattered in all directions. She crept to the cave-in and peered over.

"Don't come any closer, the bank ain't solid. Can you give me something to pull myself up with?"

"How about your fishing pole?"

One end of Kirk's sprout broke, he slipped several inches further down the bank. He gasped and closed his eyes against the pain in his leg. "Can you hold on to my pole and pull?"

"I'll try."

"Sit down and brace yourself, so you won't slip. I'm a lot heavier than you are."

Addie placed herself behind a fallen log and braced her feet on the trunk. "I'll hold out the pole, but don't bend it too much or it'll break. I'm ready. See if you can pull yourself up!"

Kirk's hands were wet and slick with mud. He turned loose with one hand, wiped it on his jacket and worked his fingers to loosen their stiffened numbness. He grabbed the big end of the cane pole and clamped down. He got his good foot lodged in a root, tested the pole and his hold held. He released his other hand and wiped it. With both hands on the pole, he dug in his good foot and pulled himself up a few inches.

"Can you hold me?"

Addie grunted. "Hurry, I can't hold you too long."

Kirk climbed one hand above the other. One hand slipped several inches. A sliver of cane joint plunged beneath the skin on his palm. He gasped and moved his hand further up. The sliver stabbed with each movement. Hand over hand, he advanced, digging with his good leg. He progressed. His forehead broke out into a sweat from the jagged pain in his leg.

"Hurry!" Addie moaned.

Kirk grabbed at an exposed root with his right hand and when it held, he moved his left hand further up the pole.

"I can see your hand, you're almost up. Come on— you're going to make it."

Kirk searched with his left hand until he found a root over the edge.

"Don't!" Addie screamed. "That one's not connected."

"Which way can I go?"

"To your right, there's a big root. Maybe you can get your fingers under it. A little further, a little more."

"Is that it?"

"Yes."

Kirk gripped the root as mud squashed under his nails and the sliver pierced into his palm. "I've got it."

"You can reach up with your other hand. There, I think you'll be fine now, let go of the pole."

Kirk released his hold, Addie's hands gave out and she lost her grip. The pole clattered down the bank and he saw it spear into the flood waters, then disappear. His stomach felt queasy, he closed his eyes, took in a deep breath, and forced his stomach to settle.

Addie stood over the log with one foot on either side and reached for his hand.

"Give me your hand."

Kirk looked up into the face of the girl that looked too small for the task. *I trusted her before, we got no choice now. I can't hold on much longer.*

Addie reached for him and Kirk placed his muddy hand in hers.

"Climb." Addie pulled as she clung to a stubby branch with her other hand. Kirk dug in his toe, lunged, and fell sprawled over the edge of the bank. Addie fell, tumbling backward over the log. Her feet came up and she disappeared from Kirk's sight. He dug a few more inches and lay his head on his arm to catch his breath. A convulsive shudder shook his shoulders, but he didn't cry.

"Kirk? Are you all right?" came a soft voice.

"Yes— I'm out of breath, just give me a minute." He

didn't raise his face for her to see his tears.

She knelt by his side and brushed the mud from his hair.

Kirk looked up and said, "Addie, you saved my life. Thank you."

Addie looked away, "Can you get up?" She pried her arm under his shoulder to help him.

Kirk tried and gasped when he moved his leg.

"My leg's hurt, I can't walk on it. Can you go get your paw to help me?"

Addie was gone, squishing up the path, before the words were out of his mouth. She hollered, "I'll be right back!"

Kirk lay back down and sobbed. His body trembled as the shock of his experience came over him. *So cold, I'm so cold.*

&

An apparition appeared at the back door of the Charlton house.

Lydia opened the door and screamed, "Addie, is that you? What happened? Are you all right?"

"Kirk fell over the bank— and I helped him out. He hurt his leg and can't walk. Can Papa come help him?"

When Douglas heard Lydia scream, he came down the stairs, two at a time, still grasping his paper.

"What's the matter?"

"Papa, you have to help Kirk! He's hurt on the path and he can't walk."

"Show me where." Douglas turned Addie around and with long strides started down the path with Addie running along side. When they turned the corner of the wall. Douglas took in the jagged bank at a glance.

"Addie, stay close to the wall."

He saw Kirk laying on the ground, sprinted to his side and knelt over the boy. He pulled the youth's sodden body further from the gaping hole.

"Kirk? Kirk, are you all right?"

The boy trembled under Douglas' hand. "I'm just tired. Can you help me get home, I can't walk by myself."

"Addie, go next to the wall, run on home. Tell your mama to bring a blanket to the back porch. I'm going to carry Kirk.

We'll wrap him up. Go on, hurry! Be careful."

Lydia paced up and down the porch staring at the corner of the wall. When Addie came into sight, a sob escaped her throat.

"Papa's coming, he said to get a blanket."

Lydia brought two blankets. She draped one around Addie and opened the other on the porch floor for Kirk.

Douglas, carrying his burden, came around the corner, splashed up on the porch and through the back door.

"Wrap him up in that, I'm taking him on home. Get Addie warm and dry." He squished away up the muddy street toward the boardwalk in front of the store.

Lydia closed the door and reached for the bedraggled little girl, "Come on, Addie. Let's get some water on to heat and we'll warm you up with a good hot bath."

They went into the kitchen. Lydia put pots and pans on the wood cook stove. She filled the pans with water and opened the stove to heap in more kindling for a quick hot fire.

Addie sat wrapped in the quilt, on a kitchen chair. She began to hiccup. She shivered.

"Momma— I was so scared. I was reading and I heard someone call for help. I just thought I heard it at first, then he called again. I went to the wall and looked over. I couldn't see him, but he yelled again. I piled Papa's wood against the fence and climbed over. Kirk's fishing pole was laying on the bank— a whole chunk was gone. He told me not to come too close. I sat down behind a log and held the pole out for him. He pulled and pulled, and I— saw his hand. He finally got his arm over the edge and I caught it. We dropped the pole and it— fell into the river. Kirk fell on the top and he was shaking. I didn't know what to do— He said for me to come get Papa and—"

Lydia smoothed the wet hair off Addie's forehead. *She needs to talk.* "There, there, Addie. You did the right thing. You saved Kirk. He's more important than his old fishing pole or anything else."

"Momma, he hurt his leg and_ he couldn't walk."

"Yes, he may have sprained it, or it might be broken, but

legs heal. It will be fine when the doctor sees to it. Don't worry, Baby."

Addie plucked at the torn lace of her skirt, "Momma, I ruined my pretty dress."

"That's fine. You have others. Kirk is better than any old dress, and— Addie, I'm so glad you're safe. You were such a brave girl. I think we ought to thank the Lord for your safety. Don't you?"

"Yes, Momma."

"Dear Father, Thank you for keeping Addie and Kirk safe. Heal his leg and keep the children from catching cold. Thank you— Amen." Lydia hid a sob in her hesitation.

The whistling teakettle began to sing and ended their conversation. Lydia turned quickly to set the big galvanized tub in front of the stove and fill it with water. She tested as she poured cool water out of the water bucket from the washstand. She helped Addie out of her ruined clothes and held her hand, as her little girl stepped into the tub.

She's so little, how did she pull Kirk to safety. Oh, Lord, You must have helped her. Thank You, Thank You.

Lydia hovered over Addie as she scrubbed the mud from the little girls legs and hands.

ಜ.

By the time Douglas returned home, Addie was fast asleep in her bed. When he came in the porch door, Lydia collapsed into his arms.

Douglas moved her higher onto the porch and out of the rain. He pulled off his shoes/

Lydia could hold back no longer. "She took such a risk. Douglas, they could have both been killed."

"I know. That's why I put the wall between the house and the river, to keep our babies out of danger. I never thought about her going over the wall to help someone. Thank God, He took care of them."

"I have already. He gave us such a blessing when He let us have her. She wasn't shy when she told me about everything that happened."

Lydia recounted the highlights of Addie's story.

"When I got to the store with Kirk, his father was furious. He started in on the boy, but after I laid the boy down on a cot, his mother took over and I got Mr. Simms outside. We had a talk and he settled down. I sent him for the doctor and when the doctor took over, Simms didn't say anymore. They got the boy cleaned up, set his leg and gave him some laudanum. He was resting peacefully when I left."

"Do you think Mr. Simms will leave him alone now?"

"I think he was subdued by the time I left, so I think he'll watch himself. The doctor was pretty hard on him too. I've suspected there might be a problem there, but I've never heard him talk like that before. A man shouldn't treat a dog the way he was carrying on to that boy!"

"What was Kirk doing on the path after all this rain?"

"He was trying to catch some fish for their supper. I think his father wanted him to go upstream, but the boy disobeyed. He may have to answer to his father when he's better."

"Well, I'm glad we are out of it and everyone will be fine. Let's get cleaned up and go to bed too. I'll take care of this mess tomorrow and wash up these things then. After you clean yourself, put that quilt in the bath water with Addie's and I'll let them soak overnight."

Douglas hung his coat on the back of a kitchen chair, rolled up his sleeves, peeled off his socks, and his muddy trousers and shirt. He washed and dried himself, then hung the damp towel back on the washstand rung.

Lydia stretched her tense shoulders and blew out the light. Douglas put his arm over her shoulder and drew her against his side. They climbed the stairs together and stopped to look at Addie and John as they passed the children's rooms.

"Who knows, this might help Kirk to stop being such a pest about our wall," Lydia whispered.

"Maybe his father will be a bit more appreciative too. The Lord can turn this into a good thing, even though it was frightening this afternoon."

"You're right, I don't ever want a repeat and I don't even want to think about it."

ﻌ

A Week Later

"Momma, do you think Kirk's better?"

"Would you like to go see him?"

"Could we?"

"Let's give him a day or two and then we'll go."

Lydia and Addie went to the store a few days later to check on the injured boy. Kirk sat in a rocking chair on the boardwalk in front of the store with his leg propped on a wooden keg. His hands were busy winding a ball of tangled string.

Addie hung back. Lydia stepped up. "It's good to see you out in the sun. How do you feel?"

"Mrs. Charlton, I want to thank you and Professor Charlton for helping the other night." He looked at Addie, "Most of all, I want to thank you, Addie. You saved my life, I probably wouldn't be here, if you hadn't heard me call for help."

Addie stepped shyly around her mother. "I think God let me be on the verandah, so I could hear you. John usually makes so much noise, we wouldn't have heard you, if he was running and having fun."

"Whoever put you there, I'm thankful."

"Did you thank God that you're safe?"

"Yes, but I need to thank your family too."

Addie looked down, "I'm glad I was there."

Lydia and Addie nodded and went into the store. When they came out, Kirk spoke to them again, "Thanks for everything."

"You get well, Kirk, that's the only thanks we need," Lydia said.

The ladies walked on down the boardwalk. Kirk watched their passage, until they dis-appeared into the back door of their home. He heard a shuffle from the door of the store.

"Don't go mooning after that— *child.*"

"I'm grateful, she saved my life." Kirk spoke quietly.

"Don't you sass me, boy!" Mr. Simms hissed. He turned back to his customers in the store with a smile. "Mrs. Jones, let me help you there. That's too heavy for you."

When he was out of sight, Kirk passed his hand over his eyes in frustration. *He hasn't changed a bit. What does it take? Lord, forgive me for the way I feel about him sometimes. I can't help myself. He won't let anything good happen around here. I need to grow up and move before I get like him. I couldn't stand myself if that happened.*

ૈ♣

Kirk wasn't able to get the ill feelings his father carried for Addie out of his mind.

"Maw, what has Paw got against Professor Charlton's girl?"

"It's a long story, Kirk and I don't know all of it. He went to St. Charles shortly after they returned from Kentucky. Your father hinted that he'd learned something very interesting about the Charlton's adopted child. He would never tell me what he learned. You could ask him, but I wouldn't. He doesn't like to be questioned."

"How have you put up with him all these years, Maw?"

His mother walked away, then spoke half to herself, "Once you have children, there isn't much a woman can do about her life. There's not a *great deal* she can do once she's married, just make the best of her situation. I don't know how to do anything other than mind this store— I don't own anything much that I can call my own, other than my children." She shuddered.

Kirk saw a side of his mother he'd never seen before. She looked at him when she realized what she'd said.

"I'm sorry, Son, I don't have any call to burden you with my troubles. Forget what I said and let's do the best we can."

Kirk recalled his mother's statements many times in the days that he waited for his leg to heal.

ﷲ

When he had regained his strength, Kirk became Addie's shadow and protector at school. In the privacy of his family, he concealed his feelings. If his father knew, he would find a way to interfere. Kirk still peeped over the wall when he passed by, but he waved when Addie looked his way.

I like the way she runs, with her dress floating out behind her and her curls. Her hair gets curlier when the river fogs come in. Somehow she's sunny, even when the sun isn't out. Ever since I fell off the cliff, she smiles at me when she sees me. She still tucks her head, but now, I know she's shy, she ain't shoddy. Don't know how I ever thought she was.

At first, he waved tentatively, but as he received her encouraging smile, he purposely made noises to catch her attention and gave a big wave, occasionally a small shout. He thought there was no one to see him, next to the river, except Addie or her brother. He didn't know that the adults in the Charlton house witnessed his little displays for attention.

"You know, Addie's helped Kirk. He acts a gentleman at the Academy now," Douglas observed from his seat in the swing.

"I've noticed that, he used to be sullen and spy on the children, but now, he waves and speaks to them. I think Addie was afraid of him for a while, but not now. She doesn't give him much encouragement, but that's her way."

"With a father like his, I'm not sure I want her to give him too much attention."

"It's sad. I think that boy is good at heart, but his father doesn't give him credit for anything. It's a shame to have a father that acts as if he doesn't like his own family. Are you able to make up for it during his lessons?"

"Maybe a little, but there's nothing like a father's approval to help a child grow up with a healthy mental outlook. I've seen the effects of love, *or lack of it*, in my students many times. It's not hard to detect."

"The family comes to church, but Mr. Simms acts so sugary and yet huffy. It kind of turns me against him, even though I try to be nice to the family and pray about my attitude toward him."

"There's something in that family that I don't understand and I've never figured out what it is. I caught a glimpse of it the day I took Kirk home when he was hurt. It wasn't good."

"Yes, sometimes, Mr. Simms is overly nice, but I catch something else in his talk." Lydia stared off attempting to grasp an answer. "He makes me uncomfortable when he looks at Addie. I catch a look on his face once in a while. I think he hates her and I don't know why."

"She's sweet, she's never had a mean thought for anyone. She's definitely never done anything to the man."

"I know, but I've seen daggers come from his eyes."

"Do you think Addie knows?"

"She's afraid of him and doesn't like to go to the store alone. I don't send her to *his* store any longer, even if it is in sight of our back door. If I need something from there, I go myself."

"Has she ever talked about it?"

"No. I didn't notice it until after Kirk fell off the cliff and she helped him."

"I saw it before that, but I couldn't believe it. I dismissed it from my thoughts," Douglas added.

"Oh, Douglas, how could anyone *not* like Addie?"

"I don't know, but because we know how he feels, we've got to protect her. She won't say anything, unless it gets really uncomfortable."

"I'm going to talk to her about it and see if she has any idea why he hates her. Kirk used to too, but he's a totally different boy since Addie helped him."

"Yes, he idolizes her, and I've seen him protect her at the Academy."

"Well, I'm glad there is one gentleman in that family. I think Mrs. Simms and her children may need a gentleman too."

ॐ

Kirk's father became suspicious and followed the boy. He caught Kirk waving over the fence.

"Don't go spying on the professor, they'll think our family is a bunch of crazies. They got a nigger and I told you to stay away from them. Boy, you'll answer for this when we get home."

The boy was shaken by his father's remark about the Cartons. He dragged his feet as he walked home, dreading the back room thrashing to come his way.

&

After that incident, Kirk had to be sure his mother asked him to run an errand in his father's hearing, before he went by the Charlton house.

⚒︎

Spies in All Directions

When Kirk reached sixteen, he waited for Addie at the entrance to the Academy and spoke to her, "May I walk you home?"

"You can walk along with us, if you want to, we're all friends," she answered

That wasn't exactly what I meant, but it's better than nothing._

Kirk walked Addie and her girlfriends home and waited impatiently for her to grow up. When she turned fifteen, he got the nerve to ask Professor Charlton if he might call upon Addie.

"She's a bit young yet. You can stay friends, but she can't receive callers." *Oh, Lord, how am I going to handle this? She's only a little girl.*

He heard a voice in his head.

How old was Lydia when you started court-ing her?

I know, but if I'd been her father, I'd have turned me down. I guess he did. I had to wait a long while.

Kirk often talked to his mother, in his father's absence.

"Mother, I'd like to marry Addie someday. She's the nicest girl I know."

"She is sweet, but your father doesn't like her. You'd better not let him hear you're interested in her, or he'll throw a conniption fit." Mrs. Simms sighed. "He's not an easy man."

"I know, but I keep praying he'll change."

"So do I."

≥♠

Kirk's father had eyes all over town. He and his cronies gossiped about the happenings in Boonville.

"Boy, what are you doing walking that— Charlton girl home?"

"She's the best friend I have."

"Well, don't let me see you with her again!"

Kirk tried to obey his father, but Addie's personality was more than he could withstand.

"Mother, I'd still like to marry Addie someday, if she'll have me."

"Shhh." Mrs. Simms looked toward the store room.

Simms stormed out the door, "What's the matter with you, Boy? You don't have to marry her. She's not what you think she is. She's a nigger!"

Kirk whirled on his father, "Don't you ever say anything against her again! Where'd you get an idea like that? She's a wonderful person and without her, I'd— probably be dead. You ought to be thankful to her."

"Haven't you heard me all these years? I said not to sass me, you thick headed sprout!" Simms raised his fist to box Kirk's ears, as he had so many times in the past. "She's a nigger ain't you heard what I've said all these years?"

"I told you never to call her that again." Kirk lashed out and struck his father on the chin. The man sat down heavily on the floor of the storeroom with his coat tails splayed around him.

Kirk continued, "I don't care what she is, I love her and I'm going to marry her someday, *if* she'll have me. She saved my life and I'll always be in debt to her."

"You're no son of mine. Get out and don't ever darken my door again, and stay away from your mother too, you nigger lover! I won't have this family tainted."

Kirk restrained himself, picked up his hat and bolted out the door.

Late that evening, his mother stealthily placed a bundle by the back door. The next morning it was gone. She hoped that her eldest son had found
his clothes and the few dollars she had saved from her sewing.

When Kirk walked toward the river, he put a note in the door of the Charlton home. *Addie, I need to leave home for a time. I'll be in touch. Keep praying for me.* He started to sign *Love*, but couldn't bring himself to put his feelings on paper for someone else to see. He looked up at the windows of the house and signed, *Your Friend, Kirk.*

He walked to the river and caught a small flatboat heading downstream. At Hermann, he went ashore and walked into the mercantile store, when he saw a sign in the window, "Clerk Wanted."

After several weeks, the storekeeper praised Kirk.

"Young man, I've never had such a good and well-qualified clerk. with the experience you possess. Continue to do well here and I'll move you up in my businesses."

Relieved to be free of the tyranny of his father, Kirk had a good boss and was at peace with his work for the first time in his whole life.

On some Sundays, he slipped back up the river to see Addie. He went through the gate in the wall and up to the verandah, where he knocked on the front door. Sometimes the whole family came out on the verandah, other times, he visited with Addie and John, or her alone.

"Do you get to see your mother and the other children?"

"Hardly ever." Kirk answered.

"That's tragic. Would you like for me to carry your mother a note?"

His face lit up. "I appreciate your concern, but I can't get you involved. She might do, or say— something to my father and he might hurt you. I couldn't stand that."

Two Years Later
Been Away Too Long

On Monday, Douglas sat with Lydia and Addie on the verandah. They watched John play ball on the lawn with several of his friends.

"Addie, would you like to go to visit your grandmother in Kentucky and go to school there?"

"I don't know, I hadn't thought about it. Are you trying to get rid of me or something?"

"No, your mother and I want you to live your own life before you settle down. You might see things in the world that you want to do and places you want to go. Now's a good time to do it, before you get tied down with responsibilities."

"What kind of responsibilities are you thinking about?"

"Oh— you might want to get married some day and have a family, or you might like to travel— or work at something— whatever you decide, we'll leave that up to you."

"I don't know if I want to go to Kentucky. Let me think about it. Mother, you were about my age when you got married. Did Papa let you live your own life before he swept you off your feet?"

Her father answered, "I think I did let her live her own life. Your Grandpa and Grandma Williams made me wait a year before they'd even let me court her."

"But how old was she? I happen to know she was younger than I am. She couldn't have lived much life outside of her family home."

"She wasn't very old, but she was grown. She was able to make me dance a jig and she knew her own mind."

"Douglas!" Lydia scolded.

He gave her a devilish grin and looked back at Addie, "I'm not saying that you're not grown, but we can afford for you to see a few things before you settle into the adult world."

"I'm not sure, but I'll think about the trip. I don't know Grandmother Charlton very well. I only remember seeing her twice. We might not like each other."

"She'd fall all over you. Ever since my little sister died, she's wanted a girl to dress and take places."

"I'm *not a doll* to be dressed and shown off!"

"I know, but you could humor her a little while. If you don't like it, you can come home. You can stay here with your old momma and papa as long as you like."

"You both are far from old. I hope I'm as young when I'm either of your ages."

Perhaps Addie's parents saw more in Kirk's visits than they cared to reveal to her.

She was taken by surprise when on his next visit, he said, "Addie, will you marry me? I've been away from my family for six months and I've managed to save enough that I think we could make it."

Tears sprang to her eyes, she hadn't expected his question.

Kirk looked into her sympathetic face.

She's an angel and I could swim in those eyes.

"I'm not ready to get married." She made a hasty decision to use the steamboat tickets that her father had tentatively booked for Wednesday.

"Papa's going to take me to school in Kentucky and I don't know what I'll do after that. I do know that I'll spend some time with my Grandmother Charlton. My family wants me to have my own life before I settle down."

"When are you going to Kentucky?" He hurried before she could answer, "I'll wait for you until you come back."

"Kirk, you're my friend, but go on with your life. I might never get married."

"I'm waitin' anyway. Please don't go before I come next Sunday."

"Papa already has our steamboat ticket on the *Hiawatha*. We're going Wednesday morning."

"Can I write you?"

"I've thought of you as my friend and older brother, certainly you may write, and I'll answer too."

He turned his back in frustration. *I don't want you to think of me as a brother!*

Addie put her hand on his arm. "Good-by. I'll be thinking about you and— I'll pray for you."

"Thanks," he turned back. "I'll be thinking of you too. Don't stay too long— I *will* be waiting for you when you get back, however long you take."

Addie's heart softened. She hated to see him go with such a dejected look.

"Wait, I'll get Grandmother's address for you. I don't know where you live, so you'll have to write me first."

I had hope when she said, "Wait." She just wants to give me an address. I want her to come with me to Hermann.

Addie hurried up the hill to the house. She ran to her mother's desk and copied Grandmother Charlton's Kentucky address on a scrap of paper.

Kirk watched her as she ran back down the lawn. *She still floats along in her white dress, ribbons, curls and all. I'll never forget how she looks, once a little girl, now an Angel. His throat got tighter and tighter. I'm losing something and I can't do a thing about it. If she goes away, she'll never be mine. I know, I can feel it.* His heart tightened in his chest. He sucked in a breath of fresh air and willed himself calm.

"Here's Grandmother Charlton's address. I hope you can read it. I was out of breath and hurried, so I wouldn't keep you from your ride."

His heart in his eyes, he looked at her face and turned away before he broke down.

"Bye."

Addie watched him as he walked down the path, raised her voice and spoke, "I'm sorry I can't make any promises."

"Watch for me on the dock at Hermann, I'll wave as you go by." Kirk lifted his hand and turned the corner, he did not look back until he was out of her sight. He looked down from the trees on the hillside. He saw her walk up the rise of the lawn toward the verandah, just as she had so many times during his youth and in his dreams.

I don't spy on you anymore, but I still like to see you floating. He watched until she disappeared up the steps and onto the verandah.

She turned as she opened the door and looked at the hillside where the path dis-appeared away from the town.

"God bless you, Kirk. I hope things go well for you and you can find happiness. I don't think it will be with me, but I pray God will provide the love you need." *God, please bless my life too as I go to Grandmother's. We don't know each other well and— I'm scared.*

Over the River and Through the Woods To Grandmother's House

Right on time, Wednesday morning, the *Hiawatha* puffed into the landing at Boonville with her steam whistle blowing. Douglas moved numerous trunks and valises into their suite and they settled for several quiet days aboard.

Addie enjoyed having Papa all to herself. They sat on the deck or strolled near the railing, enjoying the sights. Occasionally, Addie would remind Douglas of something they had seen when she was four and came up the river the first time. He was amazed that she remembered so many landmarks, but then remembered that he had expounded at great length and pointed things out to her and Lydia.

"Momma said that I was acting the *professor* when I told you both so many things as we rode our horses along. I guess I was teaching, and you learned, or you wouldn't remember so well."

Douglas was thoughtful for a moment, "Addie, do you remember your real momma?"

"Sometimes, I think I do, but then I'm not sure."

"Do you remember what she looked like?"

"I think she had hair darker than mine and— she was pretty. She wasn't very tall, maybe shorter than Momma, I mean— my momma now. It's sort of blurred, I'm not sure what I remember and what I imagine. I think she said that my first papa had light hair, kind of like mine, but I'm not sure. I never saw him. She had to leave his picture, so I couldn't see him."

"Did she say anything about your grandparents?"

"I don't think so." Addie turned to look into her father's

eyes, "Papa, why are you asking me about all this now?"

"I'm curious. All this time I thought you'd be too young to remember, but you were telling me things about our trip I had thought you wouldn't know. We've never talked much about your family and it crossed my mind that you might remember more than we thought. Maybe we made a mistake not talking about them. If we had, it might have helped you remember and I don't think you should forget, unless you want to."

"I used to think about it, but anymore— I don't very often."

"Tell me what you remember, if you want to."

"We stayed somewhere with other people when Momma was sick. Then two bad men took me away when Momma wouldn't wake up. I know now that she must have died, but I didn't know about death then. I think— Momma used to read stories to me out of a big black book. I didn't know it was the Bible then, but it must have been, because I remember stories about baby Moses and David. Momma told me about a big fish swallowing a man. That scared me and she didn't tell me that story again."

"Was there any hand writing in the Bible?"

"I think so." Momma said, "This page is very important and she'd show me a page with words on lines. She said it told where I was born and my birthday but I don't remember any of the dates— or places."

"Do you wish you did?"

"Sometimes, I'd like to remember, but I don't know if I really want to meet any of my first family. Momma wasn't happy with her old family."

"Did she say why?"

"I don't think so. She sounded kind of— *different* when she talked of home, or their parents."

Dixieland

Addie and her father, left the steamboat at the Louisville landing and walked to the Riverside Tavern and Inn. Douglas arranged to leave part of his gear and Addie's trunks in safe keeping until he could send one of the plantation's slaves from his mother's home at Fairbank.

He rented saddle horses from the livery stable and they set out. Riding along, he had time to think of his former home, dreading sight of the plantation where his father's presence had been so prevalent.

After his father's death, four years before, Douglas missed the balance his father had added to his mother's temperament. He felt uncomfortable and missed his presence more poignantly when he was in the realm where his father had lived.

He knew his brother Rob took up the slack, as far as the management of Fairbank and The Valley, but Rob was preoccupied with his own young family and the plantations. Rob could not replace their father in Douglas' heart, and he didn't expect him to.

"I'm sorry, I drifted off into thoughts of my father. I miss him more when I'm in Kentucky than when I'm busy at home. What was that you said, Addie?"

"What will Grandmother expect of me while I'm here?"

"Oh, I imagine she will give some parties and invite some of the planters and their children to visit and meet you. I think you will find that she will keep you quite busy."

"I don't want a round of parties all the time. I'd like to learn about the farms and see where you grew up. You've told me so much about the way they do things here, I can't imagine. I want to see it for myself. Momma has even told me about the cotton gin— some other things, and she's only been here, maybe five times?"

"Yes, we haven't made the trip back many times. It's a long way and with small children, it was a difficult journey."

Douglas continued, "Probably the best visit we ever had was when your mother and I were first married and we stayed a whole summer. Lydia and my mother grew fond of each other, even though they got off to a shaky start. Did your mother ever tell you about rescuing my mother when her pony ran away?"

"Yes, she's told me about it, and then, Grandmother thought she might be the right girl for you, after all. Momma said that Grandmother didn't think she was— good enough for you before that time."

"Mother is like most of the planters, she likes to be a cut above the rest of the world. She thought I should marry a plantation belle and live here forever. Running the plantation was never my style, I wanted to teach. After that disaster with Sallie McDonnell I had to go somewhere else— or go crazy. They wouldn't have given me a job around here. Even though I really wasn't divorced, the whole situation was a grave disaster to my teaching career. People would always think there was some kind of scandal and I'd have never lived it down. It was better for me to go to Franklin and start over."

He smiled, "I would never have met your mother if I'd stayed in Kentucky. We wouldn't have you and John either. I couldn't bear all that. God knew where He was sending me. He has blessed me tremendously."

"Oh, Papa, you wouldn't have known the difference if you had never met us."

"I was very bitter after Sallie. Like my mother, I needed a taste of humility. When I look back on it, God used that to change me. I'm a better man because of the experience— and He moved me to Missouri to give me the life that we have now. He always knows what's best for us, even though, at the time, we kick and rail against His direction."

"If we knew the outcome while it was happening, it wouldn't be so hard. Like when Kirk fell off the river bank. Before that time, he didn't like me and that changed."

"Do you know why he didn't like you?"

"Partly because— I think he was ashamed."

"Ashamed, what did a little boy have to be ashamed of?"

"I heard his father beating him and talking mean when Momma sent me to the store, by myself that first time. They were in the back room and I couldn't get out of the store before Kirk rushed by. I think he was embarrassed that I overheard all that."

"Yes, I can see the humiliation that might have caused him. Sometimes we take our hurt out on others, even though it isn't that person's fault."

"Before that, I smiled at him. I thought we were going to be friends when he kept looking over the wall. After I heard his father in the store, I could see by his face that he didn't like me."

"Frustration and humiliation. None of it your fault. That wasn't fair, but who says a little boy has to always be fair? He couldn't change his father and he had to live with it. Poor child, I saw that when I took him home after he broke his leg."

"Yes, he didn't really hate me— but I was little and didn't understand it for a long time. It didn't really matter after I helped him get back up the bank."

"I didn't understand it either, but I could see it in his face. I thought maybe it was because his father didn't like us for some reason," Douglas added. "I gave Kirk's father up to the Lord a long time ago. I don't know what's the matter with him, but if he wants to change, God can do it for him. It sure would be a blessing to his family if God would work on him and get through that man's thick hide— "

"Kirk wanted me to marry him. He asked me last Sunday."

"Do you want to marry him?"

"Not now, for sure— I don't know about later."

"Your mother and I knew he wanted to marry you."

"How did you know that?"

"It was obvious to us and why wouldn't he?" Douglas squeezed Addie's hand, "You are the nicest and prettiest girl he's ever met."

"Oh, Papa!"

"We didn't think you wanted to marry him now, or you wouldn't be going off to Kentucky."

"That is one reason for me going to Kentucky, but it's not the only reason."

"Why are you going?"

"I want to get better acquainted with my grandmother. Maybe this trip will help me decide. I'm not sure yet what I want to do with the rest of my life."

"Those all sound like good enough reasons. Your mother and I want you to enjoy yourself while you're here."

"I will, but that's not the main reason I came. I wanted to give Kirk some distance, and a chance to meet other girls. Besides the reasons I've already given, I'm not ready to get married. I don't even know if I've met the right man yet."

"Many of your friends are marrying. I hope you don't rush yourself, even though I don't think you will. Kirk, may have asked you to marry him out of gratitude too. That wouldn't be a good enough basis for marriage, unless there was more to it than that."

"No," Addie looked at her papa. "Would it bother you, if I decided to be a spinster lady?"

Douglas turned to see if Addie was serious. "No, if that's what you want. We want you happy. There's something to be said for being unmarried. In the Scriptures, Paul had plenty to say about staying unmarried, dedicating your life totally to God."

"I've looked at his writings and considered them."

Douglas hurried with his remark, "Don't get me wrong. I, for one, think there's much to recommend marriage too. Your mother is the best thing that ever happened to me." The two rode in companionable silence for a few minutes.

Douglas' voice came from far away, "I was very lonely before I found her."

"If I could be as happy as you and Mother, I'd get

married tomorrow." Addie reached over and put her hand on her father's where it rested on the horn of his saddle. Douglas covered her hand with his other hand and squeezed.

"I love you, Baby."

"Me, too, Papa."

"We're almost there. Do you remember what Fairbank looks like?"

"Yes, it's beautiful, but I see why you left it too. It's kind of like a humming bird. I'll enjoy it, but I don't want to hold it in my hand. It would be *fatal* if I did."

"That's an interesting thought, but I see what you mean. I'd turn it around, maybe I was the humming bird that had to fly, rather than Fairbank. I would have been smothered by the whole plantation had I stayed."

"That might be a better explanation than mine."

"There *she* is, through those trees. She is breathtaking, isn't she?"

"Yes, Papa. She is beautiful. Because I don't want to stay doesn't keep me from enjoying that beauty, *for a time*. It's like a nice painting that I don't own and that doesn't suit in my home."

"I'm ready, shall we canter up the lane?"

"Yes, let's be a little reckless, it may be my *last* chance for a few days. *Grandmother will expect me to be a lady*."

"Addie, you always did like to ride fast."

They set the saddlebreds to a fast canter, leaving dust hanging in the air over the lane. Those at the plantation heard them coming.

The Arrival

The meeting with Douglas' mother went about as he had expected. She had social events scheduled for Addie for the next six months and was already working on the second half of the year.

"Mother, stop for a minute, will you? I'm going home in a few days and I'd like to talk with you just a little before I go."

"Just as soon as I finish these notes, we'll sit on the verandah and have a long talk. Can't you be patient?"

Douglas sighed and went to join Addie where she was talking with the children who swept the yard.

"You'd better finish this conversation before Mother comes outside, or these children will be in trouble for shirking their duties."

Addie turned to him, "Do they have a school here?"

"Not in a real sense. It's illegal to teach slaves to read or write. I hadn't thought about it for a long while, but I guess it's a way to hold them in the present institution." Douglas was brought up short by the bitter sound of his last sentence. "Addie, you make me look at slavery from afar. When I lived here, I could overlook what went on, but now when I come back, it strikes me afresh and it's harder to take. Your mother always had a way of doing that. I thought it was just her, but now, I think it's from being away and looking at it differently. It makes me feel worse looking at these children. They're much like the children at Boonville. *If I gave them the opportunity*, they would be as smart as the young people I teach every term."

"Papa, I think you're right. These children play and do

what children everywhere do. I think if they had the opportunity, they would be able to read and write as well as any of us."

"I don't want you and John to ever quit seeing people as individuals. That's one thing you children have taught me."

"Can we change it here?"

"I don't know, Addie. It would be a big job. I don't think I'm up to it. I can't even convince my mother, but I don't quit trying."

"That's all we can do, Papa."

"What?"

"*Try and keep trying.*"

"I love you, Baby. Don't let Mother change you, even a little." Douglas hugged Addie to him. "I'm going to hate to leave you— in this lioness' den."

"I'm going to hate to see you go, but with the Institute, I think I'm well-armed for this cage. Maybe I can even tame these lions a little."

"I hope so, but don't be too disappointed if you can't see a change. I've worked on Mother for years and I don't think I've made much progress toward taming the beast."

Addie laughed and Douglas joined her, with a bear hug. Her grandmother sailed onto the verandah to join them.

꙳

Before Douglas left, he and his mother had a heated discussion about Addie's treatment.

"Mother, Addie's a wonderful person. Please don't try to make her over."

"Well— "

"No, well— . I think you'll find Addie has a mind of her own, even though she won't flaunt it until you get to know her better. She'll be courteous but she won't do anything against her will. Let her enjoy herself— however she desires, don't badger her with all the frivolous social affairs."

"We'll see."

Douglas sighed, "Yes, I expect we will." *At least she'll be in school part of the time. I'm glad Addie will have control over some arrangements. If Mother gets too dictatorial, she can flee back to the Institute.*

ક

Within two weeks after Douglas left, Addie did flee to the Institute, only to return every six weeks for a weekend. Even though sweet and compliant, she would not allow her grandmother to plan her time and her life, she had more important things to accomplish.

She absorbed knowledge about her favorite topic and had observed wise examples in Professor Davis and Miss Pickens. Their teaching techniques were very different, but she was fascinated by their methods. Miss Pickens, gruff and stiff, and the professor, gentle and intuitive. She found the characteristics she expected from gender to be the opposite. Both accomplished their goals, but their differences only added to her fascination.

She studied mannerisms, assignments, voice and dress, attempting to dissect how each method worked so well. She also observed their instructions, absorbing philosophy which she would adapt to her own career. More and more, Addie grew convinced that she desired to help educate children in her own classes, maybe even someday, the plantation slaves at her grandmother's.

ક

She was absorbed in her schooling, then six weeks would be past again and it would be time to visit Grandmother. Each time, she was less impressed with the lack of substance in the life expected of her in that setting. After listening to Professor Davis and Miss Pickens, she found the young planter group of less and less interest to her.

Grandmother Charlton grew frustrated.

"Addie, where are you? You seem to be way off somehere else. Why can't you come more often, then you could get into the social whirl more fully? That Institute is ruining your social standing. You're becoming— *bookish and dry.*"

When Addie smiled and said nothing, her grandmother continued.

"You're wasting your looks shut up in those old buildings

with all those stuffy teachers- and your father has influenced you."

"Yes, Grandmother. He's your son, you raised him and you love him, even though he loves his books. That's the way I am too. "

"Oh, Addie— you're exasperating sometimes."

"Grandmother, I'm not really comfortable with some of the conversation I hear. You know we don't have slaves at our house and that seems to be all that some of our guests want to converse about. "How they are going to expand, buy more, raise more crops and on and on. Or who has the fastest horse or the strongest— "

"Addie, really, you're talking like a— *farmer*."

"Well, I guess that's what I am then, if that's the way I talk. I'd like to talk about something *important*."

"The way you ride, so unladylike, I'd think you'd be interested in the fine horses around here."

"I do like the horses, but I'm not interested in dressing up fancy and going to watch a bunch of men gamble and drink at the races. I'd rather spend my time studying or— ride the horse, rather than watch."

"Addie— I don't know what to say."

Addie hugged her grandmother. "Well, just don't say anything then, let me be."

"You're as stubborn as my son."

"Thank you, that's a compliment. I'd like to be like him."

Grandmother Charlton had no answer for Addie, but that didn't stop her from scheming to *brighten* what she thought of as a very dull social life.

Discovery

Past questions about Addie's parentage plagued Douglas on his return from Kentucky. Simms had dropped hints and said injurious things about the family. *What does that man know that we don't know about Addie's background? How did he get his information?*

Douglas stopped at St. Charles and went into every rooming house asking the same questions.

"Do you remember a young woman that died in your rooming house about fifteen years ago? She had a little blonde girl with her."

"No, can't say as I do," or a similar answer came from every clerk or owner he asked.

The last possible person answered, "I've only been here a few years. You might go ask John Tyler. He and his wife Sarah used to run this boarding house."

"Where might I find these folk?"

"Go down this block and over the bridge, they're the first house on the left." The clerk pointed from the front porch.

"Thank you."

Douglas walked down the street, praying as he walked.

Well, Lord, this is it. If I don't find any answers here, I don't think there's any left. It'll be a dead end. We'll have to let it go. Help me do what is right for Addie. Bless her and Mother as they   get acquainted. May it be a happy time for them both. Don't let Mother be overbearing. I think she's mellowed, but I haven't been around long enough to test out that theory. Please let it be true in Addie's case. Thank you for our safe trip. Be with me in this quest.

*If I'm supposed to find information about Addie, please
let it happen. If not, let us all be done with it. Thy will be done.
In the name of my Savior, Amen.*

Douglas walked to the door of the small, white cottage
with a front lawn filled with flowers and butterflies.

"I guess this is it." He knocked and listened to the shuffle
of feet coming down the hallway.

A white-haired gentleman opened the door and spoke,
"Yes?"

"Are you Mr. Tyler, who used to own the Governor's Inn
down the street?"

"Yes, how can I be of service to you?"

"Did you have a young woman boarder who died in your
rooming house about fifteen years ago? She had a little blonde girl
with her."

"Let me see. I think we did. Let me ask Mother." He
turned back toward the interior of the house. "Mother, can you
come here? I have a question that I need help on."

A spry little woman wearing an apron appeared with
more speed than her spouse had shown.

"Mother, did we have a young woman with a blonde child
with her? Seems to me I remember a young woman who died at
our boarding home about fifteen years ago."

"Why, I never! Sure we did. Don't you remember? I think
I've still got her Bible around here somewhere. I saw it not long
ago in a trunk somewhere. Bring this young fellow in and I'll see
if I can find it."

Douglas' heart lurched.

Oh, Lord, what have I done? Is this according to your
will to open this up after all these years? Why couldn't Mr.
Simms let it go? Now, I may find out something I don't want to
know. Help us.

"Sit down young man, it may take Saree awhile to find
that Bible. You one of that young'uns relatives or somethin'?
Fifteen years is a long time past to be looking for someone. You
the father of the little girl or something?"

Douglas didn't know why he felt compelled to answer this

old man, but he did.

"I'm not one of the young mother's relatives, but I am a relative to her child. My wife and I adopted her and something has come up that made me want to know more. I didn't think there was any information, but I came to a feeling that maybe someone might know more about them. She's nearing nineteen now and we love her more than you can imagine. She's a wonderful person and even if I am her father, she's beautiful in every way."

"Hee, hee. You do sound like a proud papa. I'm kinda that way myself. I got a beo—ootiful daughter too. She's got hair as black as the ace of spades and a clear white skin. She is beo—ootiful and I don't know how we managed to get her. She's tall and slim. Don't look too much like us ole geezers."

"I'm glad you have a beautiful daughter. I'm sure you do know how I feel. We have a wonderful boy too."

"That so? We had three boys, but two of 'em died with the fever. That was a long time ago."

"I'm sorry that you lost your boys. We never could have anymore after our boy, but Addie and John are enough. My wife and I have a good life and we couldn't be happier. I just took our daughter to visit her Grandmother, uh—my mother, in Kentucky. I'm returning home now. Since I was passing through, I thought I wouldn't let any more time pass before I searched for her past."

Douglas heard the screech of heavy furniture from the attic and then the tapping of tiny shoes, as Sarah Tyler descended.

"Here it is. I found her. This is her old Bible. It was left in her room when they took the child and I didn't know what to do with it. There's the baby's birth date and name here and it looks like an address, but I can't quite make it out. Maybe your eyes are better than mine? Here, see if you can.."

Suddenly Douglas didn't want to read the words in the presence of even *these* good people.

"I'm sorry, I'm overcome by this. May I take the Bible and study it when I'm ready. I've taken a blow here. We thought all these years that there was no more information and were satisfied. I can't comprehend this."

"Take the Bible, it don't belong to us. If you got the child, it's hers anyways."

"I hope it's a comfort to you and don't cause no trouble," Sarah spoke prayerfully. "Young man, can we pray with you before you leave?"

"I'd like that, I've been doing some of it myself."

"Here, Paw, gather round this Young'uns and let's offer him, and his, up to the Lord."

Douglas didn't hear all the words, but he felt peace settle over his shaken spirit as he listened to the old man offering a prayer that hit the wounds in his heart. "Amen."

"Thank you, you'll never know what this has meant to me and my family. I'll let you know how this all turns out. Give me your address and I'll send you a post."

"Yes, *sir—ere Bob*, we want to know how this comes out."

Sarah handed Douglas a scrap of paper with a neat script.

They both clapped him on the back and he walked from their home with a lighter heart.

Strategic Information

Douglas' first impulse was to open the Bible as soon as he reached the sidewalk, but his second thought came too soon for him to act. *My dear Lydia and I have been in this from the beginning and I'm not opening this until I reach her. We'll share it together. Then we'll decide what to tell Addie. Better get to the docks and catch a steamer as soon as I can. I'm anxious to get home.*

After an otherwise, uneventful trip, Douglas disembarked at the Boonville dock and ran up the hill to their home.

"Lydia, I'm home." He felt like a wayward child returning after a long journey.

Lydia flew down the stairs. "Douglas, I didn't hear you open the door. We didn't expect you quite so soon, but I'm glad you're here. John is over at Andrew's house, but I can get him home if you like. He'll be glad to see you, just as I am."

"Just as you are? I hope not! Come here." He didn't have to say anymore, as his wife of almost fifteen years melted into his arms.

Breathless, Lydia stepped back. "What's that in your package?"

"Let's sit down. We need to talk before John comes home." Douglas reached for Lydia's hand.

"It's not bad news?" Lydia leaned forward.

"I don't know. I got to thinking about what Simms had hinted, and stopped at St. Charles. I asked all the old innkeepers if they had a young woman, who had a young blonde child with her and the mother died in their establishments about twelve to fifteen years ago. At the Governor's Inn, the owner sent me to the

previous owner's home. Mr. and Mrs. Tyler were most gracious
and she still had Addie's mother's Bible tucked away in a trunk.
They opened it and started to read the birth date and wanted me to
read the place, but it hit me with such a shock, that I *couldn't do
it* then. They gave me the Bible and here it is."

"What does it say?" Lydia held her breath.

"I don't know. I didn't look at it."

"What? How could you keep from it?"

"I decided we were in this together and we should
continue that way. We've been successful and happy thus far.
Might as well continue in that manner and open it together."

"Open it, quick! I just found out, but I can't wait."

"You realize this may not be what we want to hear? We
might not be able to take back this information."

"I can't think of anything about Addie that I wouldn't
want to hear. She's been God's gift to us, He won't change that,
and nothing can take her away from us. Look!"

Douglas untied the string that held the brown paper
around the Bible. He hadn't wanted to take the chance of getting
God's precious words and the information on the flyleaf wet, but
had protected it on his trip home on the damp river.

"Your hand is shaking. Do you want me to do it?" Lydia
asked.

"You can if you want."

Lydia folded back the brown paper and ran her finger
along the edge of the cover. She raised her eyes to Douglas' and
opened the page. Her eyes ranged down the lines until she reached
next to the last entry, she read, "United in Holy Matrimony,
Orville Addison Curry and Ellen Ruth Bickfords, at Louisville,
Kentucky, ten January, eighteen hundred and— *something*, it
looks like twenty two, and the last entry reads: Ruth Addison
Curry, born in Louisville, Kentucky. The date is smeared, but I
think it reads: One, twelve, eighteen twenty two. Below that is a
line for Father and it says: Orville A. Curry and on the line
marked Mother, it says Ellen Ruth Bickfords Curry. Orville is
marked as deceased with lung fever, seven, November, eighteen
twenty two."

Lydia stopped reading to comment, "That poor woman, she got married, her husband died and she had her baby all within the same year!" Tears brimmed and coursed down her face.

"Well, we know Addie was legitimate, but we don't know too much more. Her parents really are gone, but there may be someone left in Louisville."

Douglas rose and paced the kitchen floor. "I think we need to check all the Currys and the Bickfords and see if Addie has any relatives left."

"Shhh, I hadn't thought about that! What if they want her back. We can't give her up," Lydia was stricken.

"No, we won't have to give her up. We think she's almost nineteen years old, but she knows who we are and who she is. We could never lose her. She won't let it happen, I'm very certain of her."

Lydia spoke emphatically. "You're right. I couldn't stand it if I had died and my parents were never notified that they had a grandchild. We have to look. Can we go right away?" Lydia asked.

"We've waited almost fifteen years. We need to make a few arrangements. Summer is almost gone— perhaps we could get a representative in Louisville and he could do some of the preliminary work. If he finds any promising information, we could go next spring and complete the task."

"That would give us time to adjust to the situation and prepare ourselves for what we may find. Do you think Addie will want to come home before then?" Lydia asked.

"If she does, I will send someone to escort her home, but I hope she'll continue her education."

"If we have to send someone for her, perhaps they could stop at Louisville on the way and help our representative," Lydia reasoned.

"If she wants to stay for the winter, then we won't have to send anyone after her, we could go in the spring, like you said."

"I miss her already, but I hope she stays through the winter. February will be here before we know it and then we can all go together. I want her family around her when she gets the news, *what ever* it is."

"Bad news, good news? We're in this together along with the Lord. I feel He helped me find the Tilers and He approves of our looking for Addie's family. We'll have to ask Him to help us finish what we started."

Douglas was thoughtful for a moment. "I'll go downtown tomorrow and see if I can set our plans into motion. I'll speak to Mr. Bryant and let him get things moving for us in Louisville. Then I'll need to spend some time at the Academies preparing for this term."

"I am so glad to be home," he reached for Lydia's hand.

"You're not the only one to be glad that you're home, even when you bring such frightening news along with you. Douglas, hold me, please. I don't want you out of my sight again."

Douglas stood to meet Lydia in a mutual embrace.

Much later, Lydia sighed. "Welcome home, husband."
"Thanks, Mrs. Charlton. I love you."

Search

During the winter months, Lydia and Douglas often wondered about Addie's family near Louisville.

"Why didn't Addie's mother contact her family when she lost her husband?" Lydia asked.

"Maybe she did," Douglas answered.

"But why didn't they help her?"

"I don't know, maybe we'll find answers in Louisville."

They left John with his Grandfather Williams' family. Where the boy wanted to be for the summer.

This left everyone at home happy and their attention undivided for their mission. Perhaps Lydia and Douglas would have *all* they could handle in Louisville.

The couple journeyed to complete their investigation. They would meet their representative in Louisville in five days. His information would determine their next move before they met Addie at Fairbank.

Lydia and Douglas took a steamer to Louisville and after a good night's rest, they contacted Mr. Bryant's colleague.

They listened intently while the vigorous young man reported.

"I've found the Currys, they own a plantation on the river and they lost a son named Orville about the time that Addie's father would have left home. I'm sure it's the right family, but there was some kind of scandal and the family is close-mouthed. I had to talk to neighbors to get this much information. I also contacted their minister, but he's been here only a short time and knows very little about their past history. He's willing to be of service. In confidence, I did disclose our problem to him and he vowed that he would keep it to himself, unless the families asked him to intervene. His name is Matthews and he's available at anytime, should the need arise. Here's a map that I've drawn to the Curry's plantation and I've marked the parsonage where the Reverend lives."

"Is there more?" Lydia asked.

The young man nodded.

"Proceed," Douglas prompted.

"The Bickfords were harder to find, but shouldn't have been. Their land adjoins the Curry land, but there's been great animosity between the two families. I'm surprised that they have been able to reside in that close proximity without bloodshed. A confidant said that they've ignored each other the past few years and the appearances lead me to believe, they've come to some agreement to leave each other in a strained peace.

The next day, Lydia and Douglas rode rented horses from the livery stable. They began their difficult trek to see the Currys and the Bickfords.

First, they rode to the impressive Curry Plantation. They were greeted by slaves who took them into the library where Mr. and Mrs. Curry sat stiffly in their adjoining chairs.

After disclosure of their business, the Currys softened enough to attempt to explain their actions.

"We tried too hard to protect him when he was sick. He finally rebelled and left. He sent us a message that he had married and we didn't follow up on his request that we accept his wife," tears ran unchecked down Mrs. Curry's face as she explained.

The husband picked up their explanation, "Instead, we sent him a message that we wanted him back home without his wife, or he was out of the family!" He was emphatic in stating his past blunder. "We condemned ourselves by our lack of compassionate Christian character and we've regretted our actions."

"The only message we received was one that said his wife was with child and he was very ill. He asked us to please accept her into the family, should anything happen to him. We ignored his request and never heard again," Orville's mother stated.

"We've been sorry these long years. When we came to our senses, we went to their last address and found no traces of them. It's possible that they were registered under a different name or only got their mail there, because no one seemed to remember anyone of their description," Mr. Curry added.

Mrs. Curry quietly cried into her lacy handkerchief.

Douglas spoke with compassion, "Ruth died in St. Charles, Missouri, of pneumonia or tuberculosis when their daughter was four years old. We have Ruth's Bible, and their daughter."

The Currys started, surprised.

Douglas held up a hand, "We'll let her decide if she wants to meet you. If so and you would like to meet her, that can be arranged, but— we won't let that happen unless you are ready to accept her. She's wonderful and beautiful. We've loved her from the start, and won't have her hurt. You have to make up your mind before we consider exposing her to adverse feelings from her family. If you don't wish to see her, we'll not bother you again and we won't reveal the information to our daughter. It's up to you."

"Oh, please. We had lost hope that we'd ever see our grandchild and her mother," Mrs. Curry said. "Bring her as soon as possible."

Douglas added, "We are going to see the Bickfords, then we'll go to where she is receiving further education and visiting my mother. We'll ask her if she wishes to meet her two families."

Mr. Curry shifted and averted his eyes, "I think the Currys will want to see her, but I can't speak for them. It's best you go on your own. We're at peace with each other, but we'll probably never be friends."

"Oh, James, we shouldn't say that. Who knows? We never thought we'd see our grandchild either and maybe we will."

"Yes, Mother, I guess you're right." Mr. Curry cleared his throat, husky-voiced.

"Miracles do happen," Mrs. Curry exclaimed. "Would you like to see a picture of our son?"

Mr. Curry started, "I thought we destroyed all images!"

"I'm not sorry that I kept the miniature in my locket. I'll go get it from its hiding place."

ఒ

The Bickford's house was harder to locate. They lived on a dirt farm next to the river.

When Douglas and Lydia found them, he and his wife were remarkably educated farmers that lived beside an Ohio River tributary. The Bickford's story related a pretty and gentle young girl who made the mistake of falling in love with a plantation dandy. Against their will, he continued to pursue their daughter. The attraction appeared to be mutual.

"We fell on hard times and the Currys looked down on our family. Our reluctance to the union came from the lack of acceptance from his family. They were horrid to her and I saw no reason for her to subject herself to more pain because of them. We elders persisted and the two ran away," Mr. Bickfords explained.

Addie's maternal grandmother was less rigid than her husband.

"We tried to work something out with his family, even after the young people left. They would have none of it. The Currys came crying to us about two years later, but by then, we couldn't find them. We received a letter similar to theirs."

"Earlier, they threatened us if we attempted to bring the couple back here. Mr. Curry held our loans and tied our hands. I haven't forgiven them yet. We've lost our daughter for the past nineteen years," Mr. Bickfords spoke with a strong attempt at control.

Douglas picked up the conversation, "I'm sorry, but your daughter died over fifteen years ago." Douglas soothed, "We've had your granddaughter for most of her life, but unless you wish to, we won't tell her. Then it's her decision if she wishes to meet either of her set of grandparents. We're staying at the Riverside Tavern in Louisville and we'll be there for twenty-four hours. We await your decision." Douglas and Lydia rose to leave.

A stricken look passed between the parents.

Mrs. Bickfords explained, "I knew she was gone. About five years after they left, it came to me that she was in heaven. I've never questioned that revelation from God."

Douglas made no comment on her statement. Determined to stay on course, he continued with terms.

"If we hear favorably from you, we can make arrangements for you to see your grand daughter, otherwise, we'll go on our way."

Mrs. Bickfords spoke for the two. "We want to see her. I've never forgiven the Currys, but as far as I'm concerned they have nothing to say about this. We'll be there when you say."

Lydia replied, "She's not with us now, but she's close."

"If she wants to come, we'll bring her to in Louisville, in a few days. You let us know when," Douglas added.

"We'll be ready Sunday, but we don't want the Currys to know. We can meet you in town, anywhere, and at anytime that you say." Mr. Bickford's calm was cracking.

"We'll meet by the river in the park at five in the afternoon, if that's suitable with your family. I think it's best that only the immediate family attend this first meeting and that it be out of public view. The park will be quiet that time of day. After that, we'll see," Douglas was emphatic.

"You're not to hurt her, or you'll not be allowed to see her again," she's a lovely, tender young woman and we won't have her hurt further," Lydia spoke from a mother's heart.

"We understand— what's past, is past with her. We have no further animosity toward her father, or mother. They were young and in love and our families should have compromised in dealing with that. We all refused and ended up losing them completely," Bickfords replied.

"I'm so sorry that we weren't there for our daughter, when she needed us at her husband's death or when she had the baby." She wiped her eyes, "It is very difficult for me to learn that she died alone and had no one to care for her child because of our stubbornness."

"It's something we can not easily forgive ourselves."

Douglas spoke softly, "Have you taken your bitterness to

the Lord? We've found His counsel very helpful with problems we've had."

"Yes, and no. I think this is something we have to consider more fully. Thanks for your concern, Mr. Charlton." Mr. Bickfords shook Douglas' hand, nodded to Lydia, and turned back to his plowing.

"Mrs. Bickfords, do you happen to have a likeness of your daughter?"

"Yes. Our granddaughter should see it."

"If she wishes to meet, I'd like for you to bring it on Sunday. We'll be on our way and are looking forward to seeing you Sunday afternoon, *if* Addie is willing."

As Douglas and Lydia rode away, Douglas remarked, "He's a man that doesn't easily forgive himself or others. We'll have to pray for all of them."

"Do you suppose that God can bring those two families to a more civil relationship?" Lydia asked thoughtfully.

"He can do anything, but they will have to let Him."

Addie's Decision

"Addie, we were talking as we came to Kentucky about what was in your mother's Bible," Douglas said.

"Yes. I've remembered a few more things, but nothing definite."

"Do you wish to know more?" Lydia asked.

"None of it meant much to me then. Now I wish I did remember."

"Why? Do you want to know your other relatives?" Douglas asked.

"I'm not sure. You don't know anything more about them, do you?"

"Possibly."

"You said that you'd told me all about myself that you knew and that wasn't much."

"Addie, when I went home from Kentucky after our trip, I stopped at St. Charles and asked all the boarding homes and taverns if they had a young woman tenant that died about fifteen years ago, with a young blonde-headed girl."

"What did they say?"

"At first, I couldn't find anyone that remembered the two, but then at the Governor's Inn a clerk sent me to see John and Sarah Tyler. They remembered you and your momma. I went to see them and they still had your momma's Bible. They hunted it up for me and I found your parent's names and the place and date you were born."

"Where?"

"Louisville, Kentucky."

"But— I've been in school here at Louisville."

"We know, isn't that ironic?" Douglas stalled, wanting Addie to ask for information that she wished to hear.

"When was my birthday?"

"The first of December, eighteen hundred and twenty-two."

"Why, that's several months after I celebrate my birthday."

Her mother replied, "We know. You were a few months younger than we thought when we first got you. Your middle name was Addison, as was your father's, we suppose that was why your mother called you Addie."

"Well, I guess I can celebrate two birthdays. My August one feels more normal to me. I can't imagine my birthday in December. You did get the right year though. I always wondered where I got the name Addie, now I know that too."

Lydia took Addie's hand, "I'm sure it Was a term of endearment, because you apparently resemble your father in coloring." Lydia squeezed her daughter's hand, "We have some other information too. Would you like to know about your grandparents?"

"Are— they still alive?"

"Yes, they live on adjoining tracts of land, not far from Louisville," Lydia spoke softly.

"We've been to see them and they would all like to meet you, *if* you want to meet them. We told them that it would be your decision. They are honoring our wishes."

"What are they like?"

Douglas thought for a moment. He didn't want to say anything that would prejudice Addie toward her relatives.

"Both your grandfathers are gruff, but they seem to be good men and I felt they have mellowed some in their older years. Both grandmothers are softer than the men. All four of them are sorry that they didn't approve of their children marrying when they were young. The two families were from different social circles and didn't accept the other's family. They had some difficulties in the past, but now, I think they are civil to each other as neighbors but not overly friendly."

"Will we be close to where they live when we go back through Louisville?"

"We can be, if you want to. Or, we can go close, you can see where they live, then we can pass by, if that's what you want. We'll let you decide," Addie's mother said.

"I think I want to see where they live first."

"Fine, that's what we'll do when we get to Louisville. We'll drive by their homes, then stay at the Inn in Louisville. If you think you want to see them, we can arrange it. Both sets are willing to come into Louisville to meet you, if that's what you want."

"Wouldn't it be strange, if I might have already seen or met them and didn't know?"

"The whole thing is strange, but have you ever thought, that perhaps God is leading you to your family now?" Lydia asked her daughter. "I wouldn't want you to think it's God's will, because I suggested it. You pray about it and see what answer your receive. Papa and I have been praying for you and your relatives, and we will continue to do so. They will need to accept your decision and be at peace with it, whatever you decide."

¿▲·

The little family acquired a suite in the Riverside Tavern and prepared themselves for a prayerful night. Restlessness prevailed because of the immensity of the decision that Addie was to make.

The next morning, Douglas stated, "I'll ride out and bring Reverend Matthews to our inn for counsel with us. He knows both families and may be able to give you information that will be helpful to you."

The Reverend was most helpful, but did not impose his will upon them. He offered the information Addie asked about her families in a neutral manner, and gave them prayerful assistance and assurance.

After he left, Addie said, "I can see what you meant about different social circles. Grandmother Charlton pointed out those differences in the community where she lives. It seems that the planters and the farmers don't mix socially around here either. That would explain why they might not have approved of my parent's marriage, however, that would not bother me as much as it seems to upset Grandmother Charlton, and must have been a problem for my grandparents."

"Yes, our planter class around Boonville is a bit stand offish from the farmers and merchant classes. There probably isn't as much distinction as there may be here," said Lydia. She'd grown up north of the river and was aware of minor separations in her own community. "Most of our differences around home were more in the manner in which people choose to live, some with a rougher life, while many preferred to live in a Christian manner. My father works with his neighbors on their farms and I'm not aware of differences, if there are any."

"Your mother's right. Farmers are more equal around Boonville and across the river. There is more distinction where I grew up with the planters and the farmers. Your Curry grandparents are planters and your Bickfords grandparents are farmers. Their lands join and they've had some financial differences over the years. There has been some animosity over a loan, but it's a thing of the past. They are not financially involved at the present time.

Douglas continued, "Most of their differences are over wounds from the time your parents ran away and married without their approval. I suppose they may blame each other for losing their child."

"I believe it was as much one family as the other that objected," added Lydia. "I don't think one can be blamed more than the other. It's a shame they couldn't have settled their differences many years ago, but then we wouldn't have had you and even though it's selfish, I could never wish that you hadn't been our daughter." Lydia hugged her daughter and Addie reciprocated.

"I love you Momma. I can't imagine having any other parents than you and Papa. No one could have been better to me than you both have been. I'll always be grateful to God for giving me to you, no matter what the circumstances were— or will be."

"Well, I guess that's about it. Now, we'll let you make up your own mind. I think your mother and I will go for a walk before evening. We'll be back before the sun sets."

"Get some rest. Addie, we love you, no matter what."

Douglas picked up his hat, Lydia her reticule, and they strolled out the door, down the hall and out the front door. Addie closed the door softly, went to the window and watched them start up the boardwalk. When they disappeared in the distance, she knelt by the bed for a session with her Lord.

The Meetings

Mr. and Mrs. Bickfords arrived an hour before the
appointed time. They paced nervously, and impatiently, up and
down the deserted paths of the park.

"We're wearing ourselves out. Let's sit down. Maybe we
need to ask God to bless this reunion," Addie's grandmother
stated.

"I've gotten out of practice— haven't prayed for a long
time."

"I know. I got so angry when they first left, then I was
discouraged and when I felt Ruth was dead, it all depressed me. I
haven't been able to pray well since."

"I couldn't understand why God didn't send our daughter
back. We had no way of knowing she'd gotten sick and left our
granddaughter an orphan."

"Let's try to pray."

The two bowed their heads and were silent. After a few
minutes, Addie's grandfather began to murmur, words spilled
from his mouth and became understandable, pent-up confession,
abject repentance. Mrs. Bickfords reached for her husband. They
clung to each other as they cried out their past mistakes. After a
time, they leaned against each other, spent.

A young woman walked up behind them and observed the
praying pair. Reassured she quietly said, "I'm Addie, are you my
grandparents?"

Startled, they turned as one. The two devoured the serene
face of the young woman. Her grandmother regained her voice
first.

"Yes, we're Ruth's parents and your grandparents. We're
so sorry we rejected her husband and lost her."

Mr. Bickfords cleared his throat. "We'll never forgive ourselves for driving them away."

"God can forgive you," silent tears coursed down Addie's cheeks.

"He already has, but we still feel bad about our part in the dispute," Addie's grandmother said.

"Well, as Papa says, that's "water under the bridge." Can we start from right now?" Addie asked.

The pair reached for Addie at the same instant and she folded into their embrace. The three stood crying together quietly. They'd have time to talk later. Now they soaked up lost years of affection and distance.

Addie spent the next week at their home. They filled in the years that she had missed with them and her mother's childhood and younger years. At the end of the week, she was ready to meet the other grandparents and becoming eager to go home to Boonville.

Even though she enjoyed meeting her grandparents, their lives were not hers. She was ready to go back to *her* everyday life.

ॐ

The Currys were more difficult for her to come to know. They sent a carriage with a beautiful team of spirited dappled-gray horses to bring her to their plantation. Addie felt the authority of their summons even though she would have rather met them on neutral ground.

"Do you want one, or both of us to go with you?" her parents asked.

"No, you stay here and pray for me and my attitude— theirs too."

Douglas comforted her with his words. "I'll send a messenger each day and if I haven't heard otherwise, we'll come on Sunday to retrieve you."

Addie looked into his serious face. "Oh, Papa, I think I'll be ready to go home before a week is up. I'm getting very homesick for my brother, and our home in Boonville. Does that surprise you, when we see all the property the Currys and my

Grandmother Charlton have?"

"No, you've never been impressed by wealth, why should you be any different now?" Douglas assured her.

"You're right, Papa, I'll go now, so I can hurry back."

She entered the carriage with a certain wariness and fidgeted as the horses moved off. *I wish this was already over, somehow I think it's going to be— uncomfortable for someone.*

She closed her eyes and her mouth moved silently. She did not wish the coachman to overhear. *Dear Lord, help me to be charitable to my— grandparents. It must have been a horrible mistake from what Mamma and Papa have said. Please help us all to get along with each other and help them be at peace. Help me love— and forgive them. Father, I don't know what else to ask. Please take care of it for me. Thank you, Amen."*

Somehow she felt better, but the ride was too long.

The Currys duplicated their meeting with Douglas and Lydia. In the library, they sat stiffly in their twin chairs.

Mrs. Curry looked carefully at Addie. Slowly a tear leaked down her cheek and she stood. Her arms rose and spread for Addie. The young woman was touched and stepped to enfold her father's mother.

"You look very much like your father. He was blonde like you and your eyes are his. I'm very sorry we missed so many of your years and the last years of your parents. We should have celebrated their marriage together."

William Curry cleared his throat, twisted the end of his white mustache.

"Yes, we're sorry." Her paternal grandfather placed a hand on Addie's shoulder, but appeared uncomfortable.

Addie smiled and patted his hand. He broke and clutched her to his chest.

"I'm sorry, it was my fault, your grand-mother wanted to make amends, I wouldn't let her and I've always regretted it. Please forgive me?"

"I do forgive you.. Please, *forgive yourself,* I've had a wonderful family and I didn't know the difference."

"Yes, but we could have helped and— *now I'm being selfish,* but we missed out on so much."

Mrs. Curry spoke, "You know, I think we saw you with your grandmother Charlton. Were you at that ball over in Bourbon County that the McIntires gave?"

"Why yes, I was there. There were so many people to meet, I can't remember most of them."

"We saw you, but we were never introduced. You caught my eye because you do look like your father. There was a fleeting instant I saw him, then I thought myself foolish and dismissed it. I couldn't keep myself from staring at you, but others kept up a conversation and I had to hold up my end. I think my companions found me distracted."

Addie spent the week with the Currys. They couldn't do enough for her, but when Douglas and Lydia came for her, she was ready to go home.

She took portraits and memories of her parents home with her to cherish. The families promised to keep in contact and Douglas agreed to bring the entire family for a lengthier visit the next summer.

A Reckoning

The three weary travelers arrived back in Boonville to a town running rampant with rumors. Mr. Simms had been busy spreading his information. He elaborated on his latest thoughts to two male customers.

"She's been gone long enough. She was probably *enceinte* and they needed to get her out of town to prevent a scandal. You know how them high yellar gals are. Wonder what they did with the pickaninny?"

"I don't know what you're talking about, but I think you'd better keep your mouth closed when Professor Charlton gets back to town. John said they'd be back later this week and you'd better be prepared," the first gentleman customer remarked.

"I can't believe you said that about the Charltons. You know that little girl has been the picture of angelic charm all her life. She hasn't even courted, as far as I know," the other customer said. The two turned and left the store.

Adrian Simms was daunted, but his courage returned later in the morning. He made remarks to his next few male customers.

"I didn't want to hurt the family, but now that she's of marriageable age, the town families need to know. I don't know about you, but I don't want to have a grandchild from her kind. I checked into Charlton's story. She may be from Kentucky all right, but she has tainted blood. I heard all about it on the docks of St. Charles over ten years ago, but being a *good, law abiding citizen,* I didn't want to spread the story. They bought and paid for her, then they foolishly adopted her into their family. They'll be sorry yet."

One man brightened. "Is that a fact? I find that very intriguing."

Another was taken back. "I think you'd better shut your dirty mouth before Professor Charlton hears what you've said."

Lawyer Bryant was quick to pass Simms' evil thoughts on to his client when Douglas came to catch him up on their experiences in Louisville.

"We can hold Simms liable for slander, if you wish to pursue it judicially, but I wouldn't advise that. There would be too many gossip mongers interested and the rumors would spread further with the trial."

"Thank you, Mr. Bryant. I'll be seeing you later!" Douglas turned on his heel and hurried toward the door.

"Don't let this scum make you do anything rash! Douglas?"

Douglas marched directly to Simms Mercantile.

"Simms, I'm here to see you outback." He stomped straight through the storeroom and out the back door with Simms blustering along in his wake.

"Now, see here, you can't come into my store yelling in front of my customers."

"Yes, I can! I turned you over to the Lord a long time ago, but if you open your mouth one more time telling falsehoods about Addie, I'm taking you back and cramming your words down your throat, *personally*!"

Douglas' stiff forefinger emphasized each word on Simms' breastbone. Simms retreated a step at a time.

"Do you understand me?"

"Well, I had evidence— "

"*I have evidence*! I have portraits of her grandparents and parents at my house and we personally met the four grandparents. Her parents are both dead. Addie likes her grandparents, but she has no desire to live with them. She's our daughter and if you ever slander her again, I'll see that it's the last time. May God forgive you, because right now, I don't have it in my heart. Good day!"

Douglas stalked back through the store as customers gawked after him. They had inched into the storeroom to relieve their curiosity, then made a hasty retreat back into the store when they hard the Professor's "Good Day."

With incredulous faces, they glanced at each other, but down as Douglas passed.

Simms slunk back into the store, red-faced and blustering. After one look, his customers started for the front door.

He attempted a pleasantry to cover his humiliation.

"I talked to people on the dock who saw the Charlton's buy that child. They swore she was a high yellar. I had proof."

"Afraid your proof was a pack of lies."

"'Pears that way. Come on gentlemen, we got better places to go."

"Wait! Aren't you gonna listen to me?" he protested.

"I think we heard enough of your lies already. I won't be in your store again."

"Me neither."

"No, I think I'll go across the street, even if I don't get what I want."

"Heck, I'd even go down river rather than come back here."

{❧}

Douglas hadn't deliberately intended to strike against the store and the Simms family, but it worked that way. A month later, Simms sold out and during the night, slunk away, alone.

{❧}

Mrs. Simms and the children were later seen working down river at the store in Hermann where Kirk clerked.

With six pairs of trained hands, they soon owned that store. They didn't say where their husband and father went, but curious travelers reported the family seemed more at peace than before his departure.

Unexpected Arrival

"Douglas, there must be something about that Kentucky limestone water. I haven't felt like this since I was carrying John. I'm going to Dr. Keller and have him verify what I think I already know."

"Are you trying to tell me what I think you are saying?" Douglas asked.

"Yes, exactly what you're thinking. Wouldn't that be strange, after all these years of wanting more children, to be expecting another when our first two are almost grown?"

"Better late than never. I think it would be wonderful. After all, we're not so old. You're only thirty-six, we could have several more yet."

"Please, don't get carried away. Let's cross one bridge at a time. Let me find out if this is true first."

"Do you want me to go with you?"

"No, let's not get too excited yet, it might be a false alarm. We've had a few of those over the years. And after all, I am getting to be an *old* lady, it could be something else."

Douglas drew Lydia into his arms and gave her a peck on the lips.

"Whatever, I love you more than you'll ever know. No matter what happens, it will be wonderful for us as long as we're in it together and you're still here with me."

"My sentiments exactly."

"I think Addie and John might even think it was a good idea."

"Well, I'll go find out right now." Lydia gave Douglas a hug and turned to pick up her drawstring pouch.

"Good-by and walk easy, little mother."

Lydia turned back quickly and placed her fingers to her lips.

"Shhh, Douglas, someone might hear you! We don't want to say anything until I'm sure. We might make fools of ourselves and you know how this town loves rumors."

The doctor's verdict was as Lydia suspected. She was to have another child during the winter. She and Douglas savored their secret for a time.

Addie asked, "Mother, what is going on between you and Papa? You act like two love-sick scholars."

"Addie, I think it's about time that our family had a little talk. Go get your father and send him to me. Then bring John to the sitting room for our little discussion."

"Is everything all right?"

"Go on, and hurry."

Addie looked puzzled and turned to go up the stairs to do as she was bidden.

Douglas clumped down as soon as she told him that Lydia wished to see them all in the sitting room.

"What's up?"

"Addie is suspicious, I think it's time we better tell them our little secret."

"Great! I've had a hard time keeping it from them. And I think it will make them as happy as it has us. Here goes. Little Mother, come and sit by me." Douglas tucked Lydia under his arm and they sat awaiting their children.

"What's the matter? Is something wrong?" John had a stunned, scared look on his face when he arrived just ahead of Addie.

Douglas spoke first, "No, son, nothing's wrong. Everything's right in fact. After all these years of the four of us, now we're going to be five in this family."

John was speechless. *Did he look pleased or displeased?*

Addie crowed, "Papa and Mamma, you're such good parents, I always thought you needed to fill this whole house full of children! I even prayed that you would and now you are."

"Whoa, don't fill it too quickly," Lydia replied.

Douglas answered for both of them, "The Lord didn't happen to see it that way, but I guess He thought you young people both might grow up and leave us ole folks all to ourselves. He wants us to have someone around for our old age."

"You're not old. You're both just right," Addie said.

"I hope you and the good Lord are right and I expect you are. He's never steered us wrong yet," Douglas agreed.

"I don't remember John being really little. This will be such fun for us all and I'll get to help. John too. Right, John?"

"Sure, but you surprised me. I hadn't thought about having another brother or sister for so long, that now I have to get used to it all over again. I'm glad for you though. I'll be happy to help with the— baby."

As winter advanced, Douglas came for lunch each day near noon.

In mid February, Lydia rose from the dining table and put her hand to her back.

"My back is tired today, I'm going to take a short nap this afternoon."

"You feeling all right?"

"Yes, but this burden is getting heavy."

Douglas pecked her on the cheek and turned to go back to school.

"Put the towel in the window if you need us before time to come home."

Lydia awoke with a start. She stretched luxuriantly. A stitch caught at her abdomen.

"I believe that's a definite cramp, better get myself ready. Guess my backache was the first sign and I've been working on this all day."

By the time she'd bathed and put on her gown, her body felt ready for rest. She reached for the white towel on the washstand and clipped it to the windowsill.

"Stark white against the red of the brick walls outside our bedroom window. That's our sign for the new baby. Hope Douglas sees it before too long." She sighed and crawled into their big bed.

One of Douglas' students daydreamed as he looked out the window toward the rolling snow-covered lawns. *Wish I could go out there and slide down that hill.* His eyes widened. He caught the movement of the white towel against the top story of Professor Charlton's house. *I've seen towels outside their house before. Guess they're just airing their linen.*

Douglas had caught the concentration of the young man looking out the window and peered to see where he was looking. The towel caught his eye. His heart slammed into his ribs and his throat went dry. He turned to lay his papers on the desk.

"Everett Elliott?" The boy startled and snapped to attention. "I'm putting you in charge. You've only got three more minutes of this class, then it's time to go home. I expect you *all* to act as gentlemen and leave this room thusly. I'm be seeing you tomorrow. So long, Gentlemen."

When the professor was out of the room, a murmur ran through the boys.

"Why's he leaving now?"

"It's got something to do with that white towel on the side of his house. See, right there."

Everett spoke, "Quiet, I expect quiet in here. Professor Charlton put me in charge and I expect you to be quiet for another two minutes. Now get back to work!"

The boys peered in puzzlement at his sudden show of authority, but looked back at their books in a pretense of studying.

Douglas stopped to tell the headmaster that Lydia had sent him word that he was needed at home.

"Certainly, I understand. Take good care of that little one and Lydia. I expect to hear from you in the next few hours. We'll talk about tomorrow then, after we see how things go at home. Good luck!"

"Thank you, Sir, but we don't believe in luck. God's in control and he'll handle things for us."

"Sure, Douglas, you go along home."

"As soon as school is out, would you tell John, to tell his sister to hurry for the doctor and then on home. John is to go for Mrs. Williams. We'll need Lydia's mother by the time he gets back."

"Go on home young man, we'll handle this end from here. You go on." The headmaster motioned with his hands and Douglas went.

He walked as fast as he could, stomped across the back porch and into the house. No one was in sight, so he took the steps two at a time.

"Lydia, are you up here?"

"Yes, the baby is on its way."

I thought as much. I sent John for your mother and Addie for the doctor. They should be here in a few minutes. Are you all right?"

"Just like I'm supposed to be. I don't think it will be long." Lydia ended with a grunt and bore down.

Douglas grabbed for her hands and she pulled.

After several more contractions, Douglas wiped her brow with the wet cloth.

"I hope it won't be long. It's hard to see you work so hard."

"It's not bad. This is the way it's been since Eve."

"I know, but I wasn't there with Eve— or anyone else for that matter."

"Don't make jokes."

"I'm not really, I'm just a little nervous about this whole thing."

Before Lydia could answer, they heard the clatter of feet, as Addie escorted the doctor up the stairs.

The doctor spoke first in his gruff voice, "What have we here?"

Addie peeped over his shoulder.

"We're about to get this baby born," Douglas answered

for both of them.

"Well, you wait in the hallway and we'll see about getting this job over." He pulled Addie into the room, as he escorted Douglas out, and shut the door behind the expectant father.

"Addie, do you want to help me?"

"If it's all right with you, Mamma? I'd like to help."

"I'd like you here, if you want to be. But if it bothers you, you can leave any time."

The doctor spoke brusquely, "Now, Lydia, let's see how you're doing."

"Fine, mighty fine. It'll be here in the next few minutes. You didn't give me much time to get cleaned up. Glad you've already got the water up here. I'll get ready. You two hang in there for a minute."

The doctor removed his coat, hung it over the back of a chair and loosened his tie. He rolled his sleeves above the elbow and exposed his meaty arms. He opened his black bag and set it in the chair beside the bed, poured water into the basin, carefully washed his hands, then laid out his instruments. He turned back to Lydia.

"Now, I'm ready any time you two are."

"Here— we go again," Lydia grunted.

"I can see his hair."

After a few moments, Lydia asked, "How do you know it's a *he*?"

"I just call them all that."

"Oh."

"Bear down now— There, I got his face clear." He wiped a white cloth across it's face and the baby snuffled.

"Now, push. There he's out— and he's — *a she*."

The baby cried lightly, then quieted.

Lydia panted. "I thought you said he was a boy?"

"You haven't lost your sense of humor, have you woman?"

"No, and I'm not about to now."

The doctor did a quick wipe and handed Lydia her new

daughter. He turned to Addie.

"You and your grandmother can give this baby her first toilette later. Let's finish with your mother."

Addie tucked a clean blanket over the infant and stepped aside.

"Here goes," Lydia said.

After a few more moments, the doctor spoke. "Good, good. You did well, as always, Lydia. You're a good patient, level headed, I never have to worry about you screaming or fainting on me."

"Thank you, doctor."

He turned to finish up and washed his hands. He neglected to dry, but turned down his sleeves.

"I'll get Douglas soon."

A light tap came on the door.

"Yes? "

"Is everything all right in there?"

"Right as rain!"

Douglas opened the door a crack and peered in.

"Come on in, Son. You've got another— Uh, I'll let Lydia tell you."

"Douglas, come see our new daughter." Lydia held out her free hand to him and he came to her side, reached down and kissed her. Before he stood, he reached to flip back a corner of the blanket for his first look into his baby daughter's face.

"Looks just like John did, only prettier. Have you seen her, Addie?"

"Yes, Papa, I think she's beautiful. She has the prettiest little toes and fingers. Look!"

The three studied the baby as Lydia rolled the blanket back for a better look.

After a few minutes, the doctor spoke, "Well, I think that's enough for now. Douglas, why don't you two go fix Lydia some of that tea I saw on your table while I finish up here."

The two left reluctantly with Douglas' arm around Addie's shoulders and hers around his waist. She leaned into her father in her joy and affection.

The doctor turned to Lydia, "All right, let's see if this little one knows anything about nursing."

"She's already sucking my finger, I think she's a smart one." Lydia placed the baby at her breast and soon had her newborn nursing sleepily.

The doctor relaxed quietly in the peaceful room. He roused from the rocker when they heard a noise downstairs.

"Good enough. I hear Mrs. Williams down stairs. You're both doing fine now and I'll leave you in her care. She'll send one of your men if you need anything."

"Fine. Thank you, Doctor."

"I'll be seeing you both in a few days. Stay in bed until Saturday, then we'll see about getting you up a bit." He turned to leave the room and met Mrs. Williams just outside the door.

"Good day, Mrs. Williams. You're just in time to give the young lady her first bath. But first, after you've seen her, come downstairs in about five minutes. I've got a few instructions, just in case you've forgotten."

Reconciled

A couple of months later, Douglas came to a conclusion.

"Lydia, I feel badly about the difficulty I caused Mrs. Simms and the children. I'm going down river to see them on Monday. Do you and baby Sarah feel like taking a ride on the steamer?"

Addie overheard. "Papa, can I go see Kirk too?"

"If you want to. Are you sure you want to see *a Simms*?"

"I don't feel enmity toward the family and I think I've even forgiven Mr. Simms. He got financial punishment and lost his family too. I imagine he's a very lonely man. I want to see that Mrs. Simms and the children are settled and doing well by themselves. I feel somewhat responsible, we may need to help them out in some way."

"You're right, Douglas and Addie. I think it would be good if you both went to see them. John and I will wait, with Sarah, for you at home this time."

Father and daughter returned, assured after their visit at Hermann. With the Simms' problems off their conscience, Addie began to reveal her new plans.

"Papa, I think I'd like to teach at the Academies. I've arranged to talk to the directors. Wish me well."

"I'll do better than that, I'll pray for you while you're gone. Let the Lord rule. Uh— I could put in a word for you too, if you like?"

"No, I need to go on my own. Thanks, Papa. I'll be back in a bit."

Near the end of Addie's first school term, she received a letter.

Dear Miss Addie,

Please forgive me for the disservice I paid you. After a few months of being alone, I traveled to St. Charles and located the Tilers. Your family had been to see them and they spoke highly of you. I now see the error of my information. *No. My ways.* I've repented. My family has forgiven me and I now work in Kirk's store at Hermann.

My soul could rest more easily, if I could secure your forgiveness for my words against you. I spoke to a priest here and he said that the Lord would forgive me. *I feel that He has,* but I can't rest until I also have your forgiveness.

Please reply to the address below. I remain your Humble Servant,

The letter was signed, *Adrian Simms.*

"Papa, read Mr. Simms' letter. You'll find it hard to believe, but I think he's truly sorry and the Lord has forgiven him. I think I must too."

"*Let me see that*! I'm sorry, but I find anything that pompous fool says hard to believe."

Douglas read, then reread the letter. His eyes flashed over the words, then his face softened.

"I think he has truly repented. Daughter, you're a bigger *man* than I am. I'll have to work on my forgiveness." Douglas looked away, "I think I'll give him a year and then I'll go to Hermann again and see if he's still on the right path."

"Whatever you say, Papa. I love you, Momma, John and baby Sarah. My world is a happy place again. I'm so glad we can all be together as a family."

"Us too."

"You know Papa, I didn't feel quite right, hating that man."

"No, I don't think it's in your nature to hate, but I personally find total acceptance of him very difficult."

"How about Mother and I helping you forgive?" Addie entwined her fingers in her father's jacket buttonholes.

"Good idea. You two, John and Sarah can probably straighten me out."

Douglas caught his daughter to him and gave her a swift hug. Addie laid her head on her father's shoulder and hugged him back. Her arms fit comfortably around his waist.

"Papa, I liked teaching this year. I'm glad you and Momma let me go to Kentucky and see a little of the world. I'm thankful for my other families, but I'm happiest here now, doing what God wants me to and I wouldn't have missed out on Sarah for the world."

"Good. Your mother and I will have you as long as you want to stay, *and* as long as the Lord wants you here. Umh, my sweet Addie." Douglas swung her around and then sent her on her way with his eyes looking after her with the adoration that only a father has for his grown-up *child of the heart*.

The End

About the Author

Anita Gatson Allee is one of four children born on a farm
in Ralls County, Missouri.
She and her husband reside on a small farm near Versailles,
Missouri, and are the parents of two grown daughters and
five grandchildren ranging from
two to seventeen years of age.
She has a BS degree in Education from the University of Missouri
in Columbia, MO.

I pray you will be blessed by the reading of this book.

For comments, please write to
Anita L. Allee
13216 Church Road
Versailles, Missouri
65084-4722
or e-mail to: anviallee@arthlink.net

Thank you, Anita L. Allee

About the Illustrator:
Mary King Hayden, of Versailles, Missouri Royal Theater scene
designer and former art teacher.

Child